A FRESH START

CHRISTINE GAEL

1

GAYLE

Gayle Merrill trailed her fingertips across the gleaming bar as a stab of grief pierced the blessed numbness that had taken hold that morning.

How the hell had she gotten here?

Just a few months before, she had been ready to fight like hell to hang on to the business she and her best friend had built from the ground up. But that was before a long, hard winter... Before her lawyer acquainted her with the harsh reality of the no-win situation that her sorry excuse for a husband had forced her into.

"Ex-husband," she muttered under her breath.

As of yesterday, she could finally say that it was officially over. She was single. Free from Rex and the hollow marriage they'd built. It was just as well that she hadn't let the divorce drag on and on, trying to cling to something that no judge would let her have.

Wasn't it?

"Let it go, Gayle," Jo had said. *"We did it once. We can do it again. Just let it go."*

Legally, "letting it go" had been as easy as a quick phone call to her lawyer and a few signatures. But emotionally? So far, losing The Milky Thistle felt like losing a piece of herself —one of the better ones, at that.

She had tried—Lord, she had tried—but after months of fighting to hold on to The Milky Thistle, she was exhausted. Long hours of mediation had gotten them nowhere, and Rex was so bitter that he'd refused to step away. He wanted half ownership, half of the profits, and worse? An equal say in every decision going forward. Gayle couldn't live like that, fighting over every minute decision with her lazy, philandering ex-husband.

Her lawyer had advised her that she had a good chance of winning ownership of the bar if they went to court, but Rex would almost certainly be awarded half of the bar's worth, and potentially, even future profits. Gayle would have to buy him out, and she didn't have the cash to do that. Even if she used her half of the proceeds from the sale of their family home, it still wouldn't cover the amount she would owe him. Thanks to Rex's lack of steady work year after year and his poor financial decisions, their equity wasn't what it should have been.

She could have fought for another year or more as he dragged things out. Or, she could cut her losses and get him out of her life for good. And Gayle was tired of fighting. Tired of thinking about Rex, hearing his voice, seeing his stupid face. So she'd decided to sell; assuming she'd grin and bear it, they'd carve up the proceeds, and she could walk away.

But then Rex had truly twisted the knife by declaring that he wanted to buy her out...with the help of his new girlfriend and her "family money".

Gayle could have taken him to court and tried to force a sale, but what would be the point? By then, the place already felt tainted. If she was being honest, it had felt that way since the day he had confronted her about the books.

She replayed the conversation in her mind, hands fisted at her sides at the memory.

"You're spending way too much money on food," he'd said. "Grass fed beef, sourdough bread, black cod. It's a *bar,* Gayle, not a fine dining establishment. And don't even get me started on your cheese platters. When I think of the time and money that you've wasted buying stuff in dribs and drabs instead of just ordering wholesale—"

"The stuff that those companies sling is barely food, Rex," she tried to explain. "We're supporting local farmers and artisans, buying from the community—"

"It's a business, Gayle, not a charity. Good lord... you're barely making a profit on some of these dishes."

"The other dishes and drink sales more than make up for that," Gayle had said through gritted teeth.

"Sure, you're doing okay. But you could be raking it in! Don't worry, you will be. I'm going to come and make some changes around here. Your half will be even more money than you've been making on the whole place so far. Oh, and Jo's salary? Good lord, what were you thinking? There are months that she makes more than you do. That woman has got to go. If you can't be bothered to run this place right, I'll do it."

"Like hell you will," Gayle spat. "This is my bar!"

Rex had smiled at her, grimly patronizing. "Not for long."

And, for the first time in decades, Rex had made good on his word. He had worn her down until she'd folded and let him buy her out just to be done. She had gotten a decent amount of money for the place, but it felt like she had lost the past eight years of her life... more, if she counted the years that she and Jo had spent building up the catering business that had allowed them to create The Milky Thistle.

As she looked around the empty bar for the last time, years of memories washed over her. The work that she and Jo had put into this place, building a thriving business. Those early years when they were barely breaking even. Those endless days and late nights, wondering if they were going to make it.

Tears stung her eyes as she caught sight of the long wooden tables where her son, Reid, had spent most of his senior year of high school doing homework and playing games with his friends.

Those tears fell when she locked her gaze on the stunning aurora borealis mural that her daughter, Maddy, had painted.

This bar was Gayle's home, much dearer to her than the house that she had moved out of the week before. In all the confusion of the divorce proceedings, running the bar, and negotiating the legal nightmare of trying to figure out her best option when it came to The Milky Thistle, she still hadn't found a new place to live. She was staying with her youngest sister for a while... Nikki had been happy to have her, but sleeping in her niece's room at this point in her life felt humiliating.

At least at Nikki's house, she didn't feel like a third

wheel. Nikki's boyfriend lived in Bluebird Bay, so she spent most of her days at work and most of her time off with Mateo and their half-sister, Anna. Their other siblings were both navigating new relationships, and their lives were messy; Jack was trying to piece his family back together, and Lena was supporting Owen's family through a devastating loss. They had both offered, but Nikki's house made the most sense. Until Nikki's daughter came home for spring break to reclaim her room... if Gayle hadn't found a place to live by *then*, she'd have to stay with Eric. And as much as Gayle loved her father, moving back to her childhood home at the age of fifty felt even more pathetic than sleeping under a ceiling of glow-in-the-dark stars. Well, she would find a new place soon enough. It's not like she had anything else to do...

Gayle was jobless and homeless at fifty years old.

"Are we done here?" asked Jack in a gruff voice.

Gayle jumped, startled from her thoughts, and turned to look at her brother. Jack stood at the top of the stairs, casting an impatient look around the bar. The big things—including the furniture that Gayle had specially made from an old barn that had been torn down—had to stay as part of the sale.

But there were plenty of things that hadn't been included. Gayle had packed up the board games that filled the cabinets; many were games that she had bought for Maddy and Reid years ago. Jo had packed up all of her simple syrups and homemade liquors; she'd also claimed the dartboard.

There wasn't much left.

"Two more boxes," she told him. "Just there."

Jack hefted them both, one on top of the other, and

carried them down the stairs. Her twin was fit for fifty. In his prime, really. Which meant maybe she was too...

Surely, if she kept telling herself that, she would eventually start to believe it.

With one final glance at the interior of her bar, Gayle turned off the lights and plodded down the stairs.

The sun was shining and the temperature was in the fifties—positively toasty for March in Cherry Blossom Point, Maine. A good downpour would have been better suited to Gayle's mood.

"Ready?" Jack asked.

"As I'll ever be," Gayle told him.

"Where are we taking this stuff?"

"I'll put it in Dad's garage, for now."

"Roger that."

Jack opened the passenger-side door for her, and Gayle walked away from The Milky Thistle for good. Before she could climb up into his truck, Jack pulled her into a brisk, one-armed hug. After a moment of shock, she leaned in and squeezed. Gayle couldn't remember the last time she had hugged her brother, but she was positive that it wasn't in this decade, and that *he* hadn't initiated it.

Letting his ex, Corinne, back into his life and attending regular grief counseling was doing wonders for her brother. He was a bit more like the person she remembered from childhood, less like the hardened man he had been these past twenty years since his son River had passed. If Jack could heal from such a horrific tragedy and find some peace and happiness after all these years, surely, she could weather this storm?

She sucked in a steadying breath. "Thanks for being here, bro."

Jack stepped back with a grunt and circled around to the driver's side.

As he started up the engine, he said, "I have a few hours before my next class. Should we get some lunch, or...?"

"No," Gayle said immediately, stomach still roiling from the emotional roller coaster of the day. After a beat, she softened it with, "Thank you. I'm not hungry. Anyway, you know that there's always a ridiculous amount of gourmet food at Nikki's place. I won't be able to eat and then, all of a sudden, my appetite will kick in sometime before bed, and I'll eat a whole tray of truffle mac'n'cheese."

Jack took the long way around, driving along the river instead of through town. There were green plants popping up here and there, even a few flowers... the foolish things would be killed by the next frost.

"What's next?" Jack asked.

Gayle looked at him, lips set in a habitual frown. "What?"

"What's next...for you?" he asked patiently. "You're too young to retire."

"I start over. Again. At fifty." Gayle's voice was flat.

"You say it like it's ninety." Jack laughed. "A fresh start at fifty isn't so bad."

"I don't know if I have the strength to do it all again, Jack... or the courage."

"You have time, and a decent amount of money from cashing in on the house and bar. Wait it out, give yourself some time to think, if you need it. But don't just give up.

Whatever you do next, you'll knock it out of the park, just like you did with The Milky Thistle. I know it hurts now, Gayle, but getting free of Rex in every way is a good thing. You'll see."

Maybe he was right, Gayle thought. Maybe sometime down the line, she would feel grateful that she'd dodged a bullet with Rex. Maybe someday, she'd find some new passion and this would all seem like a blessing in disguise.

But today?

Today, it just hurt.

2

JACK

Jack dropped Gayle off at Nikki's after a visit with their dad, and then turned his truck homeward.

To Corinne.

The love of his life was back in Cherry Blossom Point after two decades apart. It was still surreal coming home to her at the end of the day...hard to believe that they were living together under the same roof. Only a week into their cohabitating, he struggled with an edgy fear that she would change her mind and run for the hills.

When they'd reunited over the holiday season, they hadn't been sure how they would handle the miles between them. They had spent three months trying things out long distance. Both of them had realized very quickly that they wanted more. Corinne's business was mobile, and because she specialized in grief counseling, she had a high turnover rate. She could always open an office in Cherry Blossom Point. The self-defense academy and the survival training school he ran, on the other hand, would be difficult to recreate. So when they had begun to talk about moving in together, Corinne had offered to move in with Jack.

"It's also that much closer to Providence," she'd said with a grin. Her daughter, Kiera, was in her first year of college in Rhode Island. "There's nothing really keeping me here, anyway..."

Jack could hardly believe his luck.

Not that it had been all sunshine and rainbows. It had been a long, hard, emotional winter for him. He and Corinne had worked through so many difficult conversations about their son... and had some good ones, too. Jack could look at a picture of River now without falling to his knees, though some days it felt more like bracing himself for a quick punch to the gut than avoiding the hit altogether. And there were still points when he didn't know whether he wanted to burst into tears or punch his therapist in the face. The grief counselor that Corinne had referred him to was an ex-marine, and Jack genuinely liked him. Still, dealing with the grief that he'd been holding on to for twenty years had been painful, and the wound was still raw.

The rest of his life with Corinne, though? Were smooth as silk. She was an easy woman to love.

Jack pulled into the driveway of his house—*their* house—and headed inside. He found her standing at the stove, sautéing onions and garlic. He walked up behind her and wrapped his arms around her waist. Her thick hair hung loose down her back, and he brushed a strand of it aside to kiss her neck. Corinne obliged by tilting her head slightly to one side, cheek curving into a smile. He kissed her temple and murmured into her ear, "What's cookin' good lookin'?"

"Liver and onions," she said.

Jack laughed and took a step back. He moved towards the stove for a better look at her face.

"Seriously?"

Jack had ordered liver and onions on their first date—well, their first date this millennium—and Corinne had been thoroughly disgusted.

"Nature's multivitamin, right? Isn't that what you said?"

"You're a marvel," he said, smiling down at her.

"I bought chicken livers from a local farm because that's the only kind of liver I can stomach. Eat yours whole, if you must, but I'm making mine into pâté."

"I'll take some pâté," Jack said agreeably.

"Good. I bought a huge loaf of sourdough, too, and an ungodly amount of butter."

"Sounds divine."

"There's wine, too. Why don't you open it?"

Jack pulled a bottle opener from the drawer that she had filled with all sorts of kitchen tools. "What's the occasion?"

"You don't need to have a special occasion for a good meal, my love." Corinne accepted her glass of wine with a wry smile.

She had rescued Jack from a life of canned soup and instant coffee. A life that Jack had been more or less content with until she showed up...It was like she'd led him from a prison cell into the forest. That good-enough life would feel like torture to him now. It was self-imposed torture *before*; he just hadn't admitted that to himself until he'd been through about two months of twice-weekly therapy sessions.

"How is your sister?" Corinne asked.

"She's hanging in. It's going to take some getting used to, not having the bar to focus on."

"She's strong. I know she's going to come out the other side of this better than ever."

Jack nodded his agreement as Corinne pointed to the fridge.

"I got some asparagus," Corinne told him as she began to sear the chicken livers. "Can you grab it and trim the ends for me?"

"Asparagus?" Jack protested, even as he did as he was told. "It's only March."

"Believe it or not, March is spring in some parts of the world."

"Bah humbug," he muttered cheerfully.

"Nature's multivitamin these may be, but some of us need vegetables, too."

"I eat vegetables," Jack protested. "I even forage wild vegetables. Come along on the survival school outings this spring and then you'll see. All the fiddleheads you can eat. Purslane, dandelion greens…"

"Sounds great," Corinne said. "But this isn't the eighteenth century. You can indulge in the occasional green food that you didn't grow or forage yourself. Even some fresh fruit from time to time. It staves off scurvy."

"So do fish eyes."

"What? Ew!"

"Excellent source of vitamin C. So are certain fatty glands on game animals, like moose. The adrenal glands, I think. That's how people used to get through Maine winters. They ate everything. Brains, tripe… They would even mix the lungs with—"

"Ugh, stop. I draw the line at chicken livers. If this is what your survival school looks like, I'm out."

"No." Jack chuckled. "The stuff we teach is more for emergencies, or just people who want to get back to nature on a camping trip. Temporary shelters, fires, that kind of stuff. You can just eat roasted fiddleheads. Maybe some fresh fish?"

Corinne regarded him with narrowed eyes and took a long sip of wine. "No brains?"

Jack laughed again at the look on her face. "I promise." He paused, still thinking of the fascinating books he'd read. "Did you know that succotash was originally made with bear fat and dog meat?"

"That's it. I'm out." Corinne handed over her spatula and walked away. "I'm going to get a jump on my quarterly taxes. *You* make the pâté."

"I don't know how to make pâté!" Jack protested.

"I printed out a recipe," she said without looking back. "It's there on the counter."

Easy enough, Jack thought, looking it over. The most difficult part was figuring out how to piece together Corinne's food processor; after that, it was smooth sailing.

After he had put the asparagus in the oven and assembled ingredients for the pâté, he headed down the hall in search of Corinne. The once-empty walls were now lined with pictures, his and Corinne's both. His son Wyatt, his niece Beth, Gayle and her kids, Corinne's daughter Kiera... and River. His gap-toothed grin, his perfect face. It still hurt to look at him, every time. But like a soldier with an old war wound, Jack had learned how to live with the pain.

"Dinner's ready," he said, standing in the doorway of his —their—home office.

Corinne looked up and smiled. "Good. Numbers give me a headache. I have to take them in shifts. Wine helps."

Jack laughed. "Are you sure about that?"

"Half a glass helps," she clarified. "I'm not saying I down a bottle while doing my taxes. Not that it isn't tempting..."

"Owning your own business has its downsides," Jack acknowledged as they walked down the hall. "I can't imagine working for someone else, though. Not at this point in my life."

"No, me neither."

They walked into the kitchen and Jack handed Corinne a spear of asparagus. "Cooked enough?"

"Perfect," Corinne said after a tentative bite. "We'll make a chef of you yet."

"I don't know about that. Line cook, maybe."

"I'll take it. Wow, this pâté is delicious." Corinne licked her finger clean, giving Jack thoughts that had nothing to do with dinner, and began spreading the pâté onto slices of sourdough.

"All credit goes to the head chef," Jack said. "Well, maybe a little bit of credit to me for figuring out that nightmare contraption you call a food processor."

Corinne laughed as Jack brought their wine over to the table and went back for napkins. His phone buzzed and he paused to check it. There was a text from Sadie, Wyatt's mom. A jolt of fear shot through him.

She almost never messaged him.

Wyatt got a new phone number, the text read. It was followed by a contact card.

Wyatt...Jack's seventeen-year-old, living son still wanted nothing to do with him. He had let Jack drive him to one winter ski meet before returning to his boarding school, but Jack had been a nervous wreck and it had been an awkward drive. Since then, Wyatt had barely made an effort to reply to his texts and had completely ignored the heartfelt email that Jack had sent at the urging of his therapist. In it, he'd apologized for how his grief had impacted Wyatt and their relationship and all but begged his son for a second chance. With the kid living in Europe, it wasn't like Jack could just show up and prove he wanted to be in his life. He had messed up too many times, let it lie for too long. Jack was fairly sure there was no fixing it, but Corinne insisted that he try. And so he tried, texting a few times a week, reminding him that his father would always be there... even if the kid didn't want to hear it. Maybe when Wyatt came home this summer, they could get on better footing.

A second message followed quickly behind.

If you can give it a week or so before you contact him that would be good. He asked me not to give you the new number. I'm so sorry. I know that hurts, but just give him a little more time. He'll come around.

Jack's stomach sank like a stone.

As positive as all the women in his life tried to be, it was hard to stay optimistic. He'd failed Wyatt terribly in the past. Sure, maybe things would change and Wyatt would eventually let him back in his life.

But as Jack sat down across from a smiling Corinne, he couldn't help but wonder...

What if he didn't?

3

GAYLE

Two weeks from the day she'd walked out of The Milky Thistle, Gayle found herself midway through a class called Still Life Painting for Inner Peace and questioning every choice she'd ever made that had brought her to this point.

According to the teacher who droned on and on as he weaved his way through the rows of people and canvases, though, there was no such thing as mistakes.

Clearly, he'd never met Rex.

"Painting is a lot like life. You need balance. Use those shadows to shape your work, direct the eye to the light. You *need* the darkness in order to see the light."

The rest of the class smiled and nodded like he was saying something profound. They were all standing under a pavilion in the middle of the town square, staring at a bowl of imported peaches. The whole thing left Gayle feeling like she'd rather swallow a grenade than stand here another minute. She could not for the life of her comprehend why anyone would want to stand in one place for so long. Suddenly, she realized that the woman next to her was waiting for an answer to some question that Gayle hadn't registered above the teacher's endless monotone.

"What?"

"Have you ever done a painting class before?" the woman asked again. She was middle-aged, maybe a bit older than Gayle. She'd seen the woman around, probably in The Milky Thistle a few times. Not a regular, but definitely a townie.

"No," Gayle replied. "My sisters told me to try different hobbies in order to find my Zen."

Even saying it out loud, she felt like a fraud. What did that even mean, Zen? If Zen meant being bored to tears but also inexplicably angry at *everything*—the Bob Ross wannabe of a teacher who would not stop talking, the circle of women who had nothing better to do on a weekday afternoon than stand around and paint peaches, her own damn self for paying for this stupid class—then sure, she was super Zen. Never been Zenner.

Isn't that what Zen *was*? Letting those feelings pass through her and *not* poking anyone in the eye with this paintbrush?

She was basically a Zen master.

She let out a miserable sigh and half-heartedly smeared a blob of something called "cadmium yellow" onto her canvas.

Who was she kidding?

It felt like she'd agreed to community service to avoid jail time... except what she was doing wasn't serving anybody. Maybe some actual community service would make her feel less useless.

"What else have you tried?" asked her painting-class neighbor. That woman's peaches actually *looked* like peaches. Gayle's were more like... deflated beach balls.

"I'm losing count," Gayle told her. Ticking things off on her fingers, she said, "I took a bonsai class and went home with an overpriced little tree that I'm pretty sure I managed to kill already. Something called 'cupping' that left me covered in bruises. A guided meditation that had me sitting in a musty room for sixty minutes thinking about the mess my ex-husband has made of my life. Oh! And hot yoga, which is as precisely as terrible as it sounds."

As a woman in full-swing menopause who already felt like a furnace sometimes, Gayle realized the error of her ways the minute she walked into that class, but she'd stayed the full fifty minutes out of sheer stubbornness.

The woman nodded sagely, nonplussed by Gayle's little rant. "Have you tried needlepoint?" she asked. "It's very calming."

"I'll keep that in mind," Gayle said, screaming internally.

Then again, stabbing something over and over again with a needle actually sounded pretty good right now...

The instructor paused next to Gayle's neighbor, praising her work in his endless monotone, and Gayle's mind drifted away. She looked at the peaches in the center of the circle and thought of the delicious prosecco bellinis she and Jo had featured last summer at The Milky Thistle. She thought of the enduring satisfaction of running a successful bar... of the staff that she'd interacted with all day long. All but one had quit when Gayle had told them that Rex and his girlfriend, Lisa, would be taking over. Technically, they'd been laid off with the understanding that Rex would rehire them after closing for renovations, so at least they would be able to collect unemployment.

She thought about all of those fun nights, having their

shift drink together, laughing and playing liars' poker for dollars, exchanging funny stories about the customers who had come through that night.

What was she going to do with herself now that it was all gone?

Who was she, even, without The Milky Thistle?

The instructor paused next to Gayle, and she startled back into the present. He cleared his throat.

"That's an... interesting interpretation, Gayle. Very... original. Evocative." He moved on to the next student, and Gayle stared at her painting. She had added a giant knife piercing the peach on the top of the pile.

So much for Zen.

The quiet was broken by a sharp, two-pinkie whistle. Gayle's heart leapt at the sound; she would know that whistle anywhere. She dropped her paintbrush and looked around. Jo rolled up to the curb in her beat-up convertible with the top down.

"Are you coming or what?" Jo called.

Gayle looked around the circle of confused faces and managed a genuine smile for once.

"Sorry," she murmured. "My, um, my ride is here. Gotta go. Nice to meet you. Happy... painting."

She grabbed her purse and made a mad dash for the car, abandoning her work in progress.

It felt like she'd just escaped a gulag.

"Thank you!" she exclaimed as she jumped into the car. "Oh my god, I love you."

"You too, boss," Jo said as she pulled away from the park. "Don't you even want to know where we're going?"

"Nope. Don't care. Just drive."

4

NIKKI

Mid-afternoon on a Friday, Nikki watched with satisfaction as her staff prepared for that night's dinner service. Less than three months after their delayed grand opening, the kitchen at Le Four Locavore was a well-oiled machine. They had their winter menu down to a science; each item that Nikki had created was reproducible by her staff. The food was delicious, and—with the exception of the ever-popular chocolate lava cake—each item used at least 90% local ingredients. Nikki had painstakingly sourced every ingredient herself, from the succulent pasture-raised lamb to the stone-ground wheat. They rotated through a variety of winter soups; pumpkin sage and parsnip with garlic honey were crowd pleasers.

All through the winter, Nikki used microgreens as a garnish for some much-needed fresh flavor; guests loved the bright pink amaranth and spicy wasabi sprouts. Thanks to ingenious farmers who used high-tunnel greenhouses to grow food year-round, their newest menu even included fresh greens. Customers who had been clamoring for a salad option were thrilled. The restaurant already had plenty of regulars, locals who came back again and again for their Manchego cheeseburger or scalloped potatoes.

After much trial and error, Nikki and her team had finally figured out how to make phenomenal pasta using the local flour. Tonight's special was one of Beth's favorites from childhood, a macaroni with a bright green cheese sauce, accomplished by blending in arugula and spinach. If the customers loved it as much as Nikki's daughter, they might have to make it a staple. If not, well, she'd at least use it as a special again when Beth came home for spring break.

Nikki had so many ideas for spring and summer. Roast chicken with spring garlic, lobster mac'n'cheese, panna cotta with fresh berries, ceviche with house-made potato chips... Opening a Maine restaurant with a locally-sourced menu in the dead of winter had been a triumph; taking it through the rest of the year—and years to come—would be a celebration, an ongoing ode to Maine and its farmers and fishermen.

Not that there weren't stresses and struggles. A restaurant kitchen was an intense place to work at the best of times. And the frequent bickering between the restaurant's owners, who tended to give contradictory orders to the staff, had caused frustration and confusion more than once. But Nikki was used to bickering between siblings; it was only to be expected as they got the place up and running.

Diane, who had wanted to create a restaurant called The Locavore, had decades of experience in the hospitality industry and ran the place well. Her banker brother, Denis, was a much more intrusive investor than Diane might have liked. He had insisted on having his own sign made at the last minute and calling the place *le four*—French for 'the oven'. In the end, they'd compromised just before the grand opening and called the place Le Four Locavore. Their squabbles hadn't ended there—they'd argued over everything from the number of tables to the font on the menu, and were still locked in disagreement over what to do with the acreage surrounding the restaurant—but Diane was a good manager; she kept most of the drama that her brother created in the front of the house. The kitchen was Nikki's domain and her sanctuary. Whatever else might be happening with the restaurant, the food was phenomenal.

"Hey, Chef," Maritza called. Nikki's secret favorite, Maritza was a line cook in her mid-twenties with a golden nose ring and freshly shaved head; she'd left a scant inch of jet-black hair on top. Nikki was just a little bit jealous; her thick curls were tolerable in the wintertime, but in the heat of a summer kitchen, they drove her half mad, even pulled back in a bun as they were now. She tucked a stray curl behind her ear and crossed the kitchen to stand beside Maritza.

"What's up?"

"Would you taste the sauce for tonight's special? I feel like it seems a little flat."

Nikki grabbed a spoon to taste the cheese sauce. It was a bright spring green; Mainers loved a pop of color at the end of a long winter.

"It's delicious, Maritza. Almost perfect. Just needs more salt."

"That's what I thought, but I wasn't sure."

"I was using Himalayan salt when I wrote the recipe; it's much denser than the sea salt we're using here. That's why the measurement was off. Add a spoonful at a time until it tastes right to you, and make a note on the recipe page."

"You've got it, boss."

"Thank you. Go ahead and bring a bowl out to the servers when it's ready; they haven't had a chance to taste it yet."

"Yes, ma'am!" Maritza said cheerfully.

Something about her reminded Nikki of Beth; it was no wonder she'd grown so fond of the hard-working young woman. As far as Nikki knew, Maritza hardly had a day off; when she wasn't at the restaurant, she was helping her mother run a food truck. Nikki missed her daughter terribly; she was grateful that she'd landed the job of her dreams just in time to keep her occupied while Beth was away at college.

Nikki moved down the line, mixing up a dressing for that night's salad while she kept an eye on their newest prep cook, a seventeen-year-old boy who was proving to be a careful, diligent worker. Let others say what they would about kids today; Nikki was consistently impressed. Beth had given everyone in the family a hand-knit Christmas gift, and then gone back to school, where she was acing her second semester. Jack's son Wyatt was thriving in Europe and was fast approaching a million followers on Instagram, where he posted everything from baking videos to death-defying ski jumps. Kiera was producing gorgeous drawings and sculptures at the Rhode Island School of Design. Gayle's kids were both successful in their careers. As far as Nikki could see, young people today were killing it.

"Nikki?" Diane was standing at the door, half in and half out of the kitchen. "Do you have a minute?"

"Of course." Nikki waved over another one of her staff

and told him to bottle the dressing she'd just made, then followed Diane out of the kitchen. "What's up?"

"Denis wants to talk to you about the menu," Diane said with much the same tone of voice and facial expression that a doctor might have when delivering a cancer diagnosis. Grimly compassionate, professional, and somewhat detached. "I've held him off as long as I can, but he keeps insisting. Do you have time now?"

"Sure," Nikki said. "We have plenty of time before dinner, and they can manage prep without me. What is it that he wants to talk about?"

"I'll let you two hash it out." Like usual, Diane seemed to be thinking of five things at once. "I have a wine delivery coming any minute, and I still need to fire a server who keeps getting orders wrong and then giving customers attitude when they complain. I've given that girl three second chances, but she just landed us another one-star Yelp review. She's done."

Ouch. All of the servers were sweet as could be with Nikki; she wondered which one was getting the axe. "I'm... sorry to hear that."

"Not your problem," Diane said shortly. "Denis is waiting in the front room."

The restaurant had been converted from an old farmhouse, and most of the rooms had been preserved for a cozy feel. Nikki's state-of-the-art kitchen overlooked the largest dining room; a large window allowed the guests to see Nikki and her staff at work. Denis was sitting in the window seat of the converted office up front, clicking away at his laptop. Nikki stood awkwardly for a few minutes before he acknowledged her. The afternoon sunlight glinted off of his bald head and metal-framed glasses.

"Nicole," he said at last. "Please, take a seat."

She briefly considered correcting him, but let it slide and simply sat down in the seat across from him. The man signed her paycheck—and a substantial one, at that. He could start calling her Susan, and Nikki would probably let it go. Denis closed his laptop and looked at her.

"When I was in the main room today, I saw you touch your hair when you were in the kitchen. No gloves, no pause to wash your hands. You touched your hair and went back to work. Do you know what would happen if a food inspector saw that? Or simply a customer who chose to leave a review stating that our chef doesn't follow protocol? You're meant to be setting an example for your staff."

"We're very careful to—"

"Obviously not. We can't afford any slips."

"Understood," Nikki said after a beat. Hadn't Diane said that he wanted to talk to her about the menu? "It won't happen again. Was that all?"

"That's the least of it." Denis sighed. "I'll cut to the chase, Nick. I'm liking the menu, but it's a little...boring."

The hairs on Nikki's arms rose as she swayed with sudden vertigo; it was a good thing that she was already sitting down. "Excuse me?"

"It's glorified diner fare."

"I don't understand," Nikki said. "Everything has rave reviews. Our regulars—"

"Our Yelp rating dropped below four stars today."

"But that's not because of the food," she pointed out quickly. "The food is—"

"It's not. Good enough," Denis enunciated. "I've been patient—I do realize that Diane hired you last minute and forced you to do a Maine-sourced menu in *January*—but I draw the line at green slime." He held the specials menu up in front of him, gripping it by one corner with his thumb and forefinger. "No one wants green mac'n'cheese, Nicole."

"I guess we'll see tonight," Nikki said quietly. The mac'n'cheese side dish would be a hit; Nikki was sure of it.

"Your staples aren't much better," Denis said, scanning the main menu. "Scalloped potatoes, roasted pork, pumpkin soup...it's nothing but mush. Hamburgers, macaroni and cheese... this isn't a public house, Nicole. Our prices aren't bottom dollar. They can't be, with these ingredients. And when customers pay this much for food, they expect more than a cheeseburger."

"That... it's our most popular item," Nikki protested weakly. It had taken her a full month to perfect that burger. The sourdough buns were baked fresh each morning in their kitchen, and everyone *loved* the garlic aioli and hand-cut fries. Customers ordered it again and again.

"We can do better. We *need* to do better if this place is going to survive. This restaurant is hemorrhaging money. Some loss is expected in the first year, but this... You're aware that most restaurants fail in their first year, yes? And you know that eighty percent of restaurants go out of business within five years of opening?"

Nikki nodded, not trusting herself to say anything to this hatefully patronizing little man.

"Now, I've been patient through the wintertime, but I expect to see more refinement on the spring menu. Fine dining. No mac'n'cheese. No burgers and fries. I want to see things that people can't find anywhere else in the state."

"Did you... have anything specific in mind?" Nikki asked.

He gave her a long, unfriendly look. "I'm not the chef, am I?" Denis continued to stare, as if waiting for an answer.

"No," Nikki said. *Because if you were, you would realize how stupid you sound.*

"That's your job, isn't it?" he pressed, almost like he was determined to make this as humiliating as possible.

She nodded and swallowed hard. "It sure is."

"I think what makes the most sense here is for you to tweak some of the items on this season's menu, and then get started on building the framework for the rest of the year. Five staple offerings for each season so that we can vet them way ahead of time and see if they're going to be a good fit. That way we don't run into the same problem we're running into now."

It was on the tip of her tongue to remind him that he'd tasted most of the items of this season's menu, and had approved them as well. So what had changed?

It was almost as if someone was in his ear...

Or maybe it's a bug up his ass.

She cleared her throat and managed a tight smile. "I'll get right on that."

Her brain had been so focused on menu creation for so long, she'd been looking forward to a little bit of mental downtime. But she needed this job, and she was in no position to argue, no matter how much she wanted to.

"Perfect," he said with a congenial smile, clearly appeased that he'd gotten his way. "Back to work, Nicole."

He reopened his laptop and resumed tapping on the keyboard. Apparently, she was dismissed.

"It's Nikki."

"What?" Denis asked without looking at her.

"My name is Nikki."

He glanced back at her and gave her a slow, grim smile. "Right. Well, get back to work, Nikki."

5

GAYLE

Jo drove her car up a long driveway just outside of town and parked in front of a massive old house. It was big and blocky in the way that old Maine houses often were, with regularly spaced windows and a bright red door. Two brick chimneys rose up from the roof. The wooden exterior looked well maintained; it was a handsome house.

"What are we doing here?" Gayle asked.

"Meeting a realtor," Jo said casually. She walked away before Gayle could reply. By the time Gayle caught up to her friend, Jo was talking to a chipper blonde woman in her thirties.

"Hello!" the realtor greeted her. "You must be Gayle. So lovely to meet you. I'm Sandy."

"Hi, Sandy," Gayle said, shelving her questions and confusion. Whatever Jo was up to, she'd find out soon enough.

"So, as I was just telling your partner, the property is just over an acre. You're welcome to go inside, take a look around.

I just need to make a quick call while you ladies assess and discuss."

Jo marched through the front door without a backward glance, and Gayle followed. Jo made a beeline for the staircase; she had been here before. The space was massive... too big for a house, too big for a bar... what was Jo playing at?

The second floor was one open space; prior owners had knocked out walls and replaced them with tree-trunk pillars. The original windows in the back wall had been replaced by massive panes of glass to showcase the house's astounding view. Acres of forest reached out to the sound, which was just visible in the distance.

"What do you think?" Jo asked.

"I think it looks expensive."

Jo's smile broadened. "Well, yeah. But how about this location?"

"It's gorgeous, Jo. But what...?"

"I have an idea. A concept. What if we go rustic and really woodsy? Downstairs we have a big game room, right? Not just darts and pool, but all kinds of stuff! Axe throwing!"

"Axe throwing," Gayle repeated slowly.

"It's a thing," Jo said, unphased by Gayle's skepticism. "We could have outdoor games, too. Cornhole, bocce, even archery. We'll sell locally made craft beer, maple ale, you name it."

"It's too big to be a bar," Gayle said.

"That's only half of it. Picture this space filled with tables. Commercial kitchen downstairs."

"Our servers will have buns of steel," Gayle said flatly. It was too much to take in, too big of a dream. And yet... she could see it. She could see this place filled with tables, all of their old regulars and more.

"The restaurant will be rustic, too. Focused on game and foraging. Fiddleheads and chanterelles, you know? Moose, venison, pheasant, elk, bison... I'm sure Nikki can give us some leads on chefs who would be a good fit. I have a whole business plan written up, but I wanted you to see the space first. Come downstairs and see the fireplaces."

As Gayle walked through the lower rooms of the building, she could see it all clearly in her mind's eye. A massive stone fireplace roaring downstairs, steins for beer, hammered copper mugs for drinks, rustic plates. Massive outdoor events in the summertime, stag parties and weddings...

"Hunter's Gathering," she murmured, transfixed. "Jo, you're a genius."

For the first time since she'd realized that The Milky Thistle was slipping from her hands, Gayle felt a spark of hope.

"But how...?"

"I refinanced my house," Jo said.

Gayle turned to stare at her. "You *what*?" Jo had lived in an apartment near The Milky Thistle for years, renting out the house that she had shared with her son while he was growing up. That house was her retirement plan.

"If we're really going to be partners on this, I figured I should put up some money. I can cover the down payment. Your investment would cover renovations and cost of business until we start to turn a profit."

It was a *lot*. This would be an expensive endeavor, and doing it would be sink or swim. They'd have to make it work or they would lose their seed money *and* Jo's life savings. Did she really believe they had what it took to rebuild from scratch and create something as successful as The Milky Thistle?

Hell yes, she did.

"I'm in," Gayle said. "Call the realtor back inside and tell her we'll take it."

6

LENA

"Thank you so much," Gemma said for the umpteenth time.

Lena pulled her into a hug. "Please stop thanking me. It's no trouble at all; I'd basically moved into Owen's studio anyway. I'm glad that the house is being put to good use. It's too big for me."

Lena had purchased the house over a decade ago, sure that marriage and children lay somewhere in her future. But the relationship she'd been in then had borne no fruit, despite its dragging on and on—and thank goodness. Ending that mediocre relationship was one of the best choices that Lena had ever made, because it had allowed her lifelong friendship with Owen McKenna to turn into something more. Lena was madly in love, still in the honeymoon phase after spending a cozy winter in the apartment above Owen's glass blowing studio. She was truly happy to be able to offer her home to Owen's little sister and her two boys. All of them were still reeling after the sudden death of Gemma's husband three months before.

Gemma had tried to keep going with her plans. The family had just moved from Denver to Massachusetts, and Gemma started at her new job as planned... but eventually, her grief caught up with her, and things fell apart. Her ten-year-old son, Aiden, had been expelled from his new school for punching another boy in the nose. His older brother, Liam, had withdrawn further and further into himself. There were days that Gemma couldn't get out of bed, and eventually, she had been fired from the job that had enticed her and Jerry to move their family two thousand miles across the country. Finally, she had given in to her brother's persistent pleas that she move home to Cherry Blossom Point and let him help take care of the boys.

Owen walked through the front door carrying a huge cardboard box, and set it in a corner. Aiden and Liam ran in and thundered up the stairs, jockeying for position as they went.

"I'm the oldest!" Liam shouted. "I get first pick!"

"That's not fair!" Aiden shoved him aside and ran down the hall.

"Little devils," Gemma said with weary affection. Unlike her brother, she spoke with an American accent. She had been so young when they'd moved to Maine that she hardly remembered Ireland... though Lena could sometimes hear the faintest hint of the old country—or simply the influence of Gemma's Irish family—in certain words. It came out more when she spent long stretches of time with her big brother.

"They're good boys," Owen said.

"They really are," Gemma replied. "They've been so

good to me this winter, Owen, you've no idea... So kind and thoughtful. Cooking for themselves when I couldn't get out of bed, bringing me tea." Tears of overwhelm appeared in Gemma's eyes, and she blinked them away. "It's too much to ask of young boys. It's no wonder they've been at each other's throats, skipping homework, getting into trouble at school... I feel like I'm failing them."

Owen pulled Gemma into a hug so fierce that his fine-boned sister seemed to disappear for a moment. Gemma was nearly a decade younger than Owen and Lena, only thirty-seven, but there were silver threads in her dark hair that hadn't been there at Christmas, and a worrisome sallowness to her skin. Gemma had always been so beautiful and vibrant; it pained Lena to see her this way. It must be torture for Owen to see his baby sister in so much pain and not be able to fix it for her.

"You are not failing them." Owen kissed the top of Gemma's head and released her. "But you've run yourself ragged trying to do the work of a village on your own. You're home now, and I can help more. You can rest. You have no idea how much I've missed those boys!"

"I don't want to rest," Gemma murmured as Owen went back out for more boxes. "I want to stay busy every minute of the day. I want to be distracted. I tried to keep going, but my body gave out on me. I was too sick to work, too sick to function..."

"Grief does that," Lena said, reaching out to squeeze Gemma's arm. "Why don't you come sit on the couch for a while? You must be exhausted after packing and driving up from Massachusetts. I'll make us some tea."

"You sound like my mam," Gemma said with a shaky

little laugh. "She always seemed to think that any ill could be cured with a cup of tea. I can't drink it this late in the day, though. I won't sleep a wink."

"I have herbal teas," Lena insisted. "A delicious cinnamon-orange tea, or a tulsi-peppermint. Or I have some ginger in the fridge. I could just make us a nice ginger tea with honey?"

"That sounds lovely, Lena. Thank you." Gemma sank down into the couch. She leaned back and her eyes immediately drooped closed.

Lena busied herself in the kitchen, putting thin slices of ginger root in a pot, along with cinnamon chips and dried orange peel. She could hear Owen's cheerful shouts to the boys, telling them to quit their fighting and help him unload the van. Lena pulled down two large mugs and put a generous spoonful of honey in each. When the tea was ready, she poured it into each of the mugs and brought them out to the living room.

Gemma's eyes fluttered open and she offered Lena a wan smile as she accepted the mug of hot ginger tea. "That smells wonderful, and that's not something I say much these days. I've had no appetite since Jerry died. There were times I could hardly keep anything down. I felt like I was dying myself. If it weren't for the boys…" She trailed off and bent her face over her mug to blow away the steam that rose up from the tea.

"It'll get easier," Lena said, wishing that she had something wiser, something more helpful to say.

"I thought I knew grief," Gemma said quietly. "When our da died, and our mam… but this is a different beast altogether. I'm not myself anymore."

"Give it time," Lena told her. "Let Owen and I help you with the boys."

"You've done too much already. It was hard for me to accept the house."

"It was just sitting here, Gemma, honestly. Stay as long as you like."

"I wish you would accept some rent. I may not be working right now, but Jerry's life insurance—"

"I can't take that," Lena said.

Gemma nodded slowly and took a sip of her tea. "Owen wants me to move into our parents' house."

"I know. Will you?"

Gemma shrugged. She and Owen owned the house outright. They split the rent that their tenants paid each month, and Owen's half went into a retirement fund.

"It feels like stealing from my brother. I know he wouldn't let me pay rent."

Owen had already informed the tenants, whose lease was up in about six weeks, that the house may not be available this next year. He wanted nothing more than for Gemma and the boys to stay in Cherry Blossom Point so that he could be a steady presence in their lives.

"You know he doesn't care about money," Lena said. "He cares about you. You and the boys are all the family he's got."

"And you," Gemma said.

Lena felt a flush rise to her cheeks. She had no reason to doubt Owen's devotion to her, but she couldn't take it for granted, either. These past months with Owen had been the best of her life, and their romantic relationship was so new that she was still terrified of jinxing it.

Gemma set her mug down and leaned back into the

embrace of Lena's oversized couch. It looked like she could hardly keep her eyes open.

"Why don't you lay down for a couple of hours?" Lena suggested. "Owen and I could take the boys out for pizza."

"Sure," Gemma agreed with a weary smile and a grateful sigh. "They'd love that."

Owen and the boys came through with more boxes, and Lena walked over to them.

"This is the last of it," Owen said. His voice was hearty and cheerful, as usual, but Lena could see the worry in his face. Gemma hadn't brought much; she had sold most of what they'd brought from Colorado and donated all of Jerry's clothes. They owned little more than their own clothes and whatever the boys had cared to keep. Lena wanted to pull Owen into a hug, but instead she turned to the boys.

"I hear there's a new pizza place in town with video games at every table. Should we go check it out?"

"Yeah!" Aiden said immediately.

"Grab your coats," Owen told them.

Liam walked over to Gemma. "Are you coming, Mom?"

"No, my love. I'm going to take a nap. Bring something back for me, will you? See if they have a pesto pizza, or something absolutely loaded with veggies."

"Okay."

Gemma opened her arms, and Liam bent towards her to accept a kiss on the cheek. Aiden was already outside dancing around the front yard, hanging from the branch of a tree, and asking which car they were going in. They all piled into Lena's car and drove the short distance to the pizza place.

It was a long, rectangular building with colorful murals

on the walls, Mario and Luigi driving around the corner as Pacman chased his ghosts... or was it the other way around? Inside, there were long community tables in the middle loaded with games; Connect Four and Battleship. The walls were lined with booths, each of which had its own screen and controllers. People were playing everything from early Atari games to modern games with movie-level graphics.

"This place is a seizure waiting to happen," Lena muttered under her breath. But the boys' faces were bright as they watched a teenager play some high-resolution game that had his avatar running through a snowy woodland, shooting arrows at a boar. She turned to scan the menu. "What do you want, Owen?"

"How about one meat lovers and one veggie? There will be plenty of the second one left to take home to Gemma."

"Sounds good. You and the boys choose a table. I'll get in line."

The place was almost at capacity, and the boys settled on a table with Mario Kart.

"It was our dad's favorite," Aiden explained when Lena joined them, "and all four of us can play. You can be Princess Peach, since you look like her."

"No way." Lena laughed. "I want to be that mushroom guy."

"That's Toad," Aiden told her. "I'm always Toad."

"How about the little dinosaur?"

"Liam always plays Yoshi."

"Ugh, fine," Lena said with comic disappointment. "The two cutest ones. Makes sense."

"I don't care," Liam said. "I'll be Mario."

Aiden looked stricken. "Dad was always Mario."

"I guess that makes me Luigi," Owen said.

"I'll be this turtle," Lena decided. "That'll be my excuse for coming in dead last."

"Coins make you go faster," Aiden said helpfully.

"I'll keep that in mind."

The boys left Owen and Lena in the dust, and even Liam was smiling and laughing by the time their pizzas arrived. Owen and the boys all went for the meat lovers pizza, which was loaded with Italian sausage and bacon. The veggie pizza was equally heavy with artichoke hearts, peppers, mushrooms, and red onions. Lena took a slice of each, and Aiden watched in fascination as she put one on top of the other. It was thin-crust pizza, and she held the double slice in a careful U as she ate. Aiden finished his first slice, then took one of each and put them together face-to-face like a sandwich. Sauce ran down his hands and he clutched the thing together to eat it, but his saucy smile was sun-bright.

"Genius," he declared.

Liam rolled his eyes, but Lena could swear there was some amusement cracking through.

After they'd eaten and boxed up the leftovers, Liam pulled Owen over to one of the computers to show him a game that had opened up. Lena and Aiden got themselves some snickerdoodles from the front counter and sat down to a game of checkers.

When they finally got back to the house three hours later, Gemma was sound asleep in the master bedroom.

"You boys go upstairs and get your clothes unpacked," Owen told them. "Let's let your mam rest."

"She's not our maaam, she's our *mom*," Aiden said with cheerful belligerence. "This is America, we have *moms*."

"It's because an Irish mother commands respect." Liam paused halfway up the stairs and did a mock salute. "Yes, mam!"

"No, it's because they spend so much time with their sheep," Aidan said as he pushed past him. He bleated in illustration, *"Maaaam!"*

Owen shook his head at them, but there was a broad grin on his face. Then again, there usually was. It took a lot to knock Owen down, and there wasn't a thing that could keep him down for long. He turned to Lena and put an arm around her shoulders.

"It does my heart good to have those boys so close. Thank you for opening up your home, my love. The house on Linden will be open again soon, and the place will be quiet again."

"I don't mind, really. I'm falling more and more in love with your place."

"It's the apartment you love, is it?" Owen growled playfully. He bent to kiss her, and for a moment, Lena forgot what she'd wanted to say.

"Yes," she said when she'd regained some brain function, "I'm with you entirely for access to your studio apartment."

"I knew it," Owen lamented, squeezing her tighter.

"Owen," she said quietly, "I'm worried about Gemma."

He straightened up, and his expression turned serious. "Gemma will be alright. She just needs time."

"She needs help."

"Of course she does. That's what family's for."

"Yes, but I mean that I think she needs more help than we can give her. She's in deep, Owen. I don't mean that we should rush her, but... Corrine just moved to town, and she's an expert in all this. A professional grief counselor, I mean. Maybe she could help Gemma process all of this."

Owen bent to kiss her again, briefly this time. "It's a good idea, love. I'll ask her. Or you can. Just give her a few days to settle in, yeah?"

"Of course."

"She'll be alright," he said again. But this time, Lena couldn't help but wonder if he was trying to convince himself.

7

GAYLE

The weeks since Gayle and Jo had signed the papers for their new business had gone by in a blur, and the building was filled with people working to get the place ready as quickly as possible. Many of their staff had agreed to work for them at The Hunter's Gathering, but they couldn't be expected to wait forever. Gayle and Jo had both been working eighty-hour weeks, both overseeing workers and doing much of the work themselves. Gayle had repainted the entire upstairs space, and then Jo had gone in and refinished the floors. The upstairs was close to done—minus the live-edge wooden tables and chairs that a local was making for them. The downstairs, however, was still in a state of dust and chaos.

Gayle had roughly zero time to dwell on Rex or The Milky Thistle. If the new place flopped, at least it was a blessed distraction. Jo walked by, deep in conversation with a carpenter, and Gayle gave herself a mental kick in the pants. It wouldn't flop. She wouldn't let it. This was for her *and* for

Jo. They were throwing everything they had into this venture. They were determined to make it work. It had to work.

She walked upstairs to the office space that she'd set up in one corner, and shuffled through papers until she found a list that Nikki had given her—local chefs and architects who would consult with them on how to turn the back corner of their building into a functioning commercial kitchen. They were still trying to find the perfect chef to run the restaurant, and renovations needed to start sooner than later. She was just about to make the first call when Jo came stomping up the steps, followed by a man Gayle hadn't seen before. He and Jo were dressed exactly the same, with steel-toed boots, Carhartt pants, and well-worn plaid shirts. They were even close to the same size, with Jo being just under six feet tall and the man slightly over.

Of course, that's where the resemblance ended. The man had black hair and a neatly trimmed beard, both streaked with silver. He was sturdy, solid looking, and his hazel eyes were surprisingly steady as they settled on Gayle's.

In her years at The Milky Thistle, she'd realized that people hardly looked each other in the eye anymore. They would look at their phone, the menu, their drink, or simply stare across the room as they spoke to you. People's eyes darted here and there, maybe meeting yours for a split second before flitting off again.

But *him*... his gaze was unwavering.

"Gayle, this is Kellan Hayes. Jack of all trades, master of ten."

She blinked herself out of her daze and forced herself to stand. Kellan offered his hand, and she took it. His hand was large and sturdy—not rough in the way of a man who works with his hands occasionally, but smooth, with the thick calluses of a man who's worked every day of his life.

"Pleased to meet you," Gayle said.

Kellan gave her a subtle, inscrutable grin. "Likewise."

"I called Kellan when I was writing up the business plan for Hunter's Gathering," Jo told her. "He hunts deer—moose sometimes—and I wanted to ask him how feasible it was to source enough wild game for a restaurant. He's also the one who's going to get us set up with the axe throwing. We were just looking at the space downstairs where it's going to be."

"So, just to clarify," Gayle said, "you want to let people throw axes... *inside* of a bar? That doesn't seem a little... insane... to you?"

Kellan chuckled. "Most things that people do seem a little insane to me."

"It'll be a hit, Gayle," Jo insisted. "I'm telling you. When we can get away for a night, I'm going to take you to that place I was talking about down in Portland. They're crazy popular, and they don't have anything going for them *but* axe throwing."

"But is it safe?" Gayle pressed. "Darts are bad enough. Remember that time you had to pull one out of Frank's shoulder?"

"It'll be fine, you'll see. It's like a shooting range or like... batting cages. All segmented off so the axe can't possibly hit anyone."

"How do you even throw an axe? Does it go spinning end over end like a dagger? How many people have the strength for that? Are they *miniature* axes?"

"You should throw a few yourself," Kellan said. "Get a feel for it. I have a setup at my cabin if you don't want to go all the way down to Portland. You could try it out, see the different types of axes I have and the targets I've made. Jack's been up a few times. He really enjoyed it."

Gayle laughed. Of course, Jack knew this guy. "My brother also enjoys doomsday prepping and eating canned goods straight from the can."

Kellan gave her a slow grin beneath his beard and said, "Enjoying and tolerating are two very different animals. I can tolerate most things, but the things that I *enjoy* are few and far between."

Gayle found herself wondering what types of things he *did* enjoy... and to her surprise, she found herself agreeing. "I could come out this weekend." *...to see your axes.* Which was definitely *not* a euphemism. Gayle bit back a giggle.

"Saturday," Kellan said firmly. "I'll be home around noon."

"Sure. See you then."

Kellan went over to her desk and wrote his address on a scrap of paper. He extended his hand again, and Gayle took it. Heat crept up her neck—hopefully not another hot flash coming on.

"It's a date," he said.

A what?

But Kellan was already walking away. As he disappeared down the stairwell, Jo let out a low whistle.

"I have zero interest in a man mucking up my life, but I gotta say... He's a looker, that one."

"He is that," Gayle admitted, "but see how slow he walks? It's more of a mosey. Like he's got nowhere to be. Way too laid back for my taste...if I was looking for a man, which I am *not*."

"Who needs 'em?" Jo said with a solemn nod.

"Not me, that's for sure."

But all the rest of the day, through phone calls and paint swatches and meetings with their contractor, Gayle's mind kept drifting back to Kellan Hayes...

8

JACK

Corinne was bouncing around the house like a pinball, trying to make sure that everything was perfect for her daughter. Kiera was on her way up from her college in Rhode Island now, driving the beater of a car that her father had given her as a going-away present. Kiera only had one week off for spring break—contrary to their Christmas plans, it was *not* the same week that Jack's niece Beth had off from *her* school, but the girls were looking forward to attending Jack's survival school over their summer break—and she would be spending half of it with her father and half-brothers. She'd called from a restaurant in Portland, and she was due any minute.

Jack's house...or, *their* house, rather, looked completely different than it had a month ago. It was filled with houseplants, and the dark brown couch was now covered in colorful pillows and soft blankets. The walls were bright with photos of Kiera and River, along with those of his nieces and nephew. Never together, of course... it still twisted Jack's guts that they would never meet. But then again, Kiera would never have existed if River had survived. Neither would his second son, Wyatt. You had to take the bad with the good; there was no separating the two. As hard as it was to see River's beautiful face, there was a strange comfort in seeing photos of their boy along with the rest of the family. There was even an old polaroid of Jack and Corinne as kids, Corinne smiling brightly into the camera while Jack kissed the side of her face; he'd been surprised that she still had it after all these years.

"Are there enough blankets on her bed, do you think?" Corinne fretted.

"Didn't you just put a fourth quilt in there?" Jack asked with a grin.

"Air mattresses can be so cold." She had purchased a two-foot-tall air mattress and set it up in their office, complete with brand new pillows and every quilt they owned.

"I think she'll survive."

"You think I'm being ridiculous." Corinne walked to Jack and buried her face in his chest. He wrapped his arms around her and held her close for a minute before she leaned back to look up at him. "And maybe I am. A little. It's just that Kiera's never stayed here before, has never even *seen* me with someone other than her father. I mean, she knows that I dated a bit, but she never met them. I never met anyone I liked enough to introduce to my daughter; it always just petered out."

"It's not as if Kiera and I are strangers." Jack had spent all of December training with Kiera daily, giving her the confidence she needed to go back to college after experiencing an assault the summer before.

"No, she loves you. It's just... a different dynamic, you know? It was just the two of us for so long. Three people in one house just feels odd to me, now. But it's fine. It'll be fine."

A honk sounded as Kiera pulled up out front, and Corinne ran to greet her. Jack gave them a few minutes before he joined them. They were talking a mile a minute, catching up on the longest period of time they'd spent apart since Kiera was born —and that was *with* Corinne driving down to spend a few days in Providence in early February. Kiera popped the trunk of her car, and Jack walked out to help with her bags.

"Jack!" As soon as she saw him, Kiera ran up and gave him a hug. Jack froze in surprise for a second, and then hugged her back. It was wonderful to see her looking so happy and confident... a far cry from the shell-shocked girl he'd met just four months ago.

"So you're happy down in the Ocean State?" he asked.

"It's been so much fun. I've been working like crazy, but I'm keeping up with all of my classes. Just barely." After Kiera had been attacked, the school had made a special exception for her and allowed her to defer for a semester. Now, she was taking a heavier course load than most students in order to catch up. She'd be caught up by the end of the year, since some of the community college courses she'd taken as a teenager would count towards her credits.

"And you like your classes?" Jack asked.

"Yeah! My teachers are amazing. We have studios three days a week—Drawing, Design, and Spatial Dynamics—and then I'm taking three, like, normal college classes too. There's The New England Landscape, which started with natural history and then went into how native people managed the landscape by doing prescribed burns to preserve grasslands or caring for trees like the American chestnut so that there was always plenty of food, and then into colonists and farmers and all, and now we're getting into the post-industrial landscape and tourism and everything. And then I'm taking two other classes. Comparative Vertebrate Anatomy is wicked awesome, but Concepts in Mathematics is kicking my butt. It's the best math class I've ever taken though. Way beyond just numbers on paper."

Jack had never heard Kiera talk like this, all in a tumble, like Beth did. *This* was the Kiera that Corinne told stories about, the one who had chatted gamely with locals in a broken mix of Italian and Spanish and French and English as they'd traveled through Europe, the one who'd made instant friends of anyone they'd crossed paths with in their months of backpacking... the one who had been scared into hiding by the assault she'd experienced just before her eighteenth birthday and coaxed out again this past winter. It was no wonder Corinne missed her so much; she shone star-bright.

Thank God nothing had happened to her and Beth last December. Jack and Corinne and Nikki had each been terrified when the girls had gone missing, and so relieved when Gayle had picked them up walking down the side of the highway at midnight. Teenagers... It was no wonder some fathers had heart attacks in their fifties.

Kiera continued to chatter, filling them in on months of excitement as if she and her mother didn't talk on the phone most weeks and text nearly every single day. Jack absentmindedly slipped an arm around Corinne's waist as they all stood in the faint spring sunshine, and Kiera smiled.

"You two look good together," she said, "like those hot old couples in Viagra commercials."

Jack barked with laughter as Corinne's face turned bright pink. "Kiera!"

"What?" Kiera laughed. "It was a compliment."

"Let me help you with your bags," Jack said. He hefted them from her trunk—an utterly ridiculous amount of stuff for a one-week vacation, but he supposed they were heavy with textbooks and art supplies—and carried them through to the office. Kiera followed, carrying a smaller bag she'd grabbed from the passenger seat.

"Your mother wanted you to have your own space," Jack said, "so the office is yours for the week. But she's also worried that you'll freeze to death on an air mattress, so you're welcome to move to the couch in front of the fire, if you'd like."

Kiera laughed. "I'll be fine here. There are enough quilts to bury me alive. I could always sleep on top of some of them if the bed is cold."

"Good thinking." Jack turned to go.

"Hey, wait. How is my mom holding up with me gone? Is she okay?"

Jack turned back to face her and smiled gently. "Corinne's great. She was worried the first month or so, but ever since she drove down to visit and saw how much you love it there, she's been fine. She's so proud of you, and she's getting used to it now."

Kiera let out a sigh of relief. "Thank you for being there for her. I'm glad she's not alone."

"There's no place I'd rather be," Jack assured her. "Are you hungry? Your mom bought all of your favorite foods."

"I just ate in Portland," Kiera laughed, "but yeah, I guess I could go for a snack."

She followed him through to the kitchen, walking slowly as she took in the pictures that filled the walls. They sat on the couch as Corinne carried out a tray of food and drinks and set it on the coffee table. She settled onto the couch between Jack and Kiera, leaning into him as she turned to ask her daughter about school. There was a fire crackling in the fireplace, and it occurred to Jack that this house had never felt more like a *home* than it did at this moment. Jack was only half listening, Kiera's chatter blending with the quiet noise of the fire, but he tuned in when he heard the words "self-defense".

"Your classes helped me a lot," Kiera told Jack when he turned his head to look at her. "I don't feel afraid anymore. I mean, no more than a normal person... I showed some of my roommates the moves that you taught me, and my friend Destiny really wants to come to Cherry Blossom Point over summer break to study with us. She and Beth are going to be best friends, I just know it."

"I'm so happy to hear that," Corinne said. "And how about the coffee shop? Do you like it?"

"I love it. I'm so busy with classes that I had to cut back to ten hours a week, just Saturdays and Sundays in the mornings. But it's so much fun. Everyone on campus goes there, so I basically know every student now, at least by name. Even the ones who aren't in my classes or my building. And I'm learning how to make so many fun drinks. The spending money is good, too. With you and Dad spending a fortune on tuition and books and art supplies, I feel more like a grownup when I can at least earn my own money for movie tickets and stuff.

"But what about you?" she asked her mom. "How has it been trying to start your practice up again?"

"Well, I haven't had to start entirely from scratch," Corinne said. "I'm still meeting with most of my patients on video calls. But I do miss working with people in person. I've found a space to rent in town, and I've already started work with a handful of clients. I think I'll be able to build up a local practice by the end of summer. I've been thinking of offering some support groups, as well—group therapy."

"That's a great idea, Mom."

They had a cozy evening at home—dinner, some multi-billion-dollar superhero movie, and ice cream in front of the fire—and then Kiera retired to her room to get some reading done before bed.

"I set my alarm for your early morning class," she told Jack as she went down the hall and called over her shoulder, "don't leave without me!"

Jack and Corinne had both been up predawn, and they were ready for bed. Corinne laid her head on Jack's chest and fell asleep almost immediately, comfortable in the knowledge that her daughter was just downstairs. They were so close, and their relationship seemed so *easy*... so far from the relationship that he had with his seventeen-year-old son, Wyatt.

Jack's relationship with River had been like that... easy. River had seemed to think that his dad walked on water, and Jack had felt much the same way about him. River had been the center of his world, his north star... there had been no barriers between them. Jack hated feeling as if there was a wall between him and Wyatt, but there always had been. Even when he was River's age...even when he was a toddler, their relationship had never been easy. Wyatt had been such a fearless, wild child. And, of course, Jack hadn't been the same man that he'd been before the death of his first son. He wanted nothing more than to keep Wyatt safe. Even at a young age, though, Wyatt had responded to Jack's every command by doing the exact opposite of what he was told. And the older he got, the more adventurous he'd become. Slowly but surely, Jack had unintentionally started to distance himself from Wyatt. Almost like his heart and mind wanted to drive a wedge between them in case he lost Wyatt the way he'd lost River. Eventually, he'd succeeded and had lost him anyway.

He'd have given anything to go back in time and do it again. With his son all but grown and living thousands of miles away now, Jack wondered if he would ever be able to fix what he had broken.

Therapy had led Jack to some profound realizations. His therapist had a way of guiding Jack to his own epiphanies rather than lecturing or preaching, and Jack appreciated that. He understood now that he had loved River with his whole being, and that after River's death, he'd pulled in tight to protect what remained of his shattered soul. When Wyatt was born, Jack hadn't been capable of loving him in the same way. There had been a cage around his heart that he hadn't even known was there, and it needed to be dismantled piece by piece if he was ever going to repair his relationship with Wyatt.

Corinne was helping. Her gentle, steady presence, her ability to laugh and make him laugh. He loved her, no question. And Kiera was amazing, as dear now to Jack as his own nieces and nephews. But there was a huge hole in his life, and he would never be truly happy until he figured out how to mend things between him and Wyatt.

Sleep felt unattainable, so Jack slipped gently away from Corinne and pulled on a sweater. He padded down to the living room and opened his laptop. When Jack went to YouTube, his history was nothing but dozens of videos of Wyatt's death-defying stunts. Jack clicked one at random. It started on his son's face, pink-cheeked and beaming as he described a specific black diamond slope, then switched back and forth between go-pro footage and shots captured by a drone as Wyatt raced down the slope.

Jack both loved and hated watching his fearless boy do these crazy feats, but these days they were the only glimpse he ever had of his son. It shook him to his core, imagining how one wrong move could send Wyatt crashing into a tree. At the same time, he was in awe of Wyatt's skill and his passion for the sport. Wyatt completed the course, and the video went back to a closeup shot of his face, laughing and joking... so different that the shuttered young man who spoke to Jack with such contempt.

Jack would bring it up again this week in therapy. And then he would talk to Wyatt's mother, Sadie. He needed to create a plan of action. Wyatt would be home for Easter in a few weeks, and Jack couldn't let that opportunity pass him by.

"I'm going to fix this, kid," he said to the boy on the screen. "I swear."

9

GAYLE

Kellan's house was a good half hour outside of town. Gayle's GPS crapped out about halfway there, leaving her to find his place the old fashioned way. She was buzzing with nerves by the time she parked in front of the small wooden cabin, and felt annoyed that she was nervous at all. Kellan came out onto his broad, deep front porch as Gayle walked up the path. He gave her a slow smile that made her stomach flop.

"It's good to see you again," Kellan said, extending his hand in greeting. Gayle took it, overly aware of how much bigger his hand was than hers. He wasn't an unusually tall man, but he was solid. Big hands, big feet... *pull it together, Gayle.* Her hand was still in his, a touch that was fast exceeding the bounds of a normal handshake. Kellan's hair was damp, and he smelled like a fresh shower.

"Likewise," said Gayle as she pulled her hand away.

"Can I give you the grand tour?" he asked.

"Sure." Gayle's heart flitted erratically as she followed

him inside. It was a comfortable space, roomier than it looked from the outside. There was a huge stone fireplace on one side of the room and a wood-fire stove on the other. Stools near a massive butcher-block counter suggested that it served as his table, as well.

"I built the place myself," Kellan said evenly. A simple statement of fact. "Felled a few trees, got most of the wood from an old house down the road that was being torn down. That's where these floors came from."

"It's a beautiful home," Gayle told him.

"Come see the root cellar."

Gayle followed him back outside, where he walked across the porch and down a second set of steps. His house was set into the hillside, level with the ground in front but far above it in back. There was a huge workshop below the house, overlooking the forest. He paused to show her some things that he was working on: a rocking horse for his neighbor's baby, a tray patterned intricately with inlaid wood, and a series of wooden bowls. Behind the workshop, set into the hillside and under the earth, was his root cellar. It was full of food, most of it packed away in boxes filled with straw or wood shavings. Rows of shelves were filled with canned tomatoes, pickles, and other preserves. It was beautiful.

"This is amazing," Gayle said. "It reminds me of my grandparents' house."

Kellan chuckled. "Jack said the same thing."

Gayle thought back to Kellan's comment of *It's a date*. But he'd given Jack the same tour. So he hadn't meant anything by it. Just as she'd thought. He'd meant an appointment, a date on the calendar... right? Right. So why was she still a bundle of nerves?

"Jack must have been impressed," she said, simply for something to say. "You might be the only other person in town who's set up to ride out the apocalypse."

"We're not in town," Kellan reminded her in his quiet, friendly way, "and there are more preppers out here than you'd think. Plenty of people don't want to be dependent on twenty-step supply chains for their basic needs. But honestly, I think most of us keep at it because it just *tastes* better. It's a hell of a lot more satisfying—on every level—than buying packaged crap at a grocery store. Here." He pulled a few jars down from a shelf and set them on his work table. "Take these home with you and then try and tell me they're not more delicious than anything you can buy in a store. But first, you should come meet my girls."

"Your *what*?" Gayle said, but Kellan was already out the door. He could move fast, for a moseyer... Gayle hurried after him as Kellan walked past a chicken coop and into the woods.

"Here, ladies!" he called. A huge white dog came bounding up, and Kellan patted him on the head.

"Hey there, Dog. Where are our ladies at?"

"Your dog's name is Dog?" Gayle asked.

"His name is Augustus," Kellan replied, still scanning the forest, "but he answers to Dog."

There was a faint chorus of bleats and clucks, and two nanny goats came walking through the forest, followed by a small flock of hens. Most of them were black, blending into the shadows of the forest, until they passed through a sliver of sunlight that bounced off their feathers in deep shades of iridescent purple and blue.

"Victoria and Beatrice," he introduced the goats as one

butted him gently, demanding attention. "Mother and daughter. My retired milkers. We used to have a little herd—that's why I got Dog's mom and dad, to keep the foxes and coyotes away—but I sold most of them off when my wife died. That was always her job, the daily milking and cheese making and whatnot. I like hunting and fishing too much to be here every day. Too much milk for me anyhow. No one wanted to buy these old girls, so they stayed. They don't mind if I drop some hay in the barn and leave for a while, and the hens have got an automatic door on their coop. They go in at night all on their own. You know what's good for you," he said to the hens, "don't you?"

A multicolored little chicken responded with a musical series of clucks. She was an unusual-looking chicken, with a red wattle, tan chest, and variegated gray feathers everywhere else. The feathers on her head went up a good inch or so, giving her a messy bouffant. She circled Kellan's boots, scratching in the dirt in search of food.

"Do you eat the chickens?" Gayle asked.

Kellan held a finger to his lips and shook his head. "Don't even let Muriel hear you say that. She'll be pissed at me for weeks. I swear she hides her eggs in the forest when she's mad at me, and the rest follow suit. Then, I have to put up the electric fencing and keep them in the yard until they start behaving themselves again. And I'll do it again," he said sternly, looking down at Muriel, "if you so much as *look* at my tomatoes this summer."

Gayle pursed her lips, holding back a giggle. "I thought you were a hunter?"

"I am. And a fisherman. And a gardener. I like to know where my food comes from. I respect nature, and I like to work with her. But these girls are my buddies. They provide me with eggs. The goats are straight-up pets, at this point, but at least they give me good manure for the garden."

Kellan led her back up the hill, stopping to open a side door on the chicken coop.

"Look here," he said. "They have three nests, but they all lay in the same damn one."

"Those are beautiful," Gayle said in astonishment. Nestled in the hay were eggs of every color. Sky blue, pink, chocolate brown, golden, jade, teal...

"Heritage eggs," Kellan said. "Muriel's a cream legbar, that's the blue. Marans lay the dark brown. When you cross the two, you get olive eggers—those are all the shades of green there. I used to breed olive eggers, but I got tired of killing the roosters off every year."

"I'm struggling to understand how you're a hunter," Gayle teased gently.

"I take a buck with reverence and it feeds a village," Kellan said as he collected the eggs. "I'm not squeamish. But killing the boys that I saw as fluffy little chicks and watched Muriel raise so carefully... I didn't much like that. Taking a life weighs the same whether it's a buck or a bird, and the roosters were barely worth eating. But if you don't cull them, they fight each other to death. I just keep hens now. It's simpler."

"They're beautiful birds," Gayle said, "and those eggs are amazing. They look like Easter eggs."

"Wait til you see the inside," Kellan told her. He locked the coop back up and carried the eggs up towards the house. "The yolks are straight-up orange, nothing like those pallid yellow things you buy in stores." Once inside, he put the eggs in a carton and handed it to Gayle.

"But you gave me so much food already," she protested. "Let me pay for these, at least."

"You want to pay me now, but you'll hate me after you eat one. You'll be ruined for store bought eggs forever," he said with a grin. "Don't say I didn't warn you."

Gayle smiled and ducked her head, somewhat unnerved by the way he looked her right in the eye when he spoke to her. "I'll keep that in mind." She glanced at a ticking clock on the wall and was shocked to see that she had already been there for over an hour, just chatting and faffing around. "Where did the time go? I have a million things to do and I'm sure you do, too. We should get to the axes."

Kellan shrugged and smiled. "I imagine we all have things waiting on us to fill our time, but I don't much worry about that. This is what I'm doing now, and I'm enjoying myself. Are you?"

Gayle stared at him for a moment, caught by the full focus of his hazel eyes. They were mostly green, flecked with gold and brown. She swallowed and nodded, feeling a spark of irritation at how easily the man could derail her thoughts. "I really do need to get back to work soon."

Kellan nodded amiably. "Go ahead and put those eggs in your car. I'll get the jars from downstairs so you don't forget them."

He met her by her car a minute later and led her out to the barn, where he had transformed one corner into a small axe-throwing course. There were axes of various sizes and well-used targets.

"Ready?" Kellan asked. "Pick one."

Gayle picked up one of the smaller axes and looked at him uncertainly. "How do I...?"

"I'll demonstrate." Kellan picked up one of the heavier axes. "You can throw with one hand or two."

"Like this?" Gayle asked, mimicking the way he held his axe in one hand. It was lighter than axes she had held before, with a much smaller, thinner head.

"Don't hold it too tight," Kellan told her. "You're getting ready to throw the thing, not chop wood or hit a baseball. Grip it lightly." He tossed his axe almost without looking at the target; it hit the center of the board and stuck.

"Now, come a bit closer," he said. "These axes are built to go about twelve feet. If you stand back that far, it'll over rotate. You'll hit with the wrong side and it will just bounce off. Face the target head on. You want to stand straight."

Kellan's hands touched Gayle's hips gently as he moved her to stand squarely in front of the target. He smelled amazing, like hay and sawdust and old-fashioned soap. She swallowed and tried to focus on the task at hand. Holding the axe in front of her face, she threw it like Kellan had shown her... and it hit the target! Not far from Kellan's axe in the center.

"You're a natural," Kellan said. Gayle grinned at him and reached past him for another axe. As her shoulder brushed his chest, he said in the same cheerful, casual tone, "You smell good."

Gayle could feel her face go bright red, and when she tried to throw the second axe, it went way off target. Who said stuff like that out loud? That was bizarre. There were *rules*. Gayle took a deep breath, trying to get her composure back. Kellan offered her another axe, and she paused for a careful inhale before she threw it. Like the first, it hit the target and stuck.

"I think I get the idea," Gayle said. "Can you build something similar for the bar? Jo wants four throwing stations separated by some kind of walls or fencing."

"I can do that."

"How long will it take you to build?"

Kellan shrugged. "I'll come in every day starting Monday and I can work eight hours or so. Beyond that, I can't say. It will take as long as it takes. But I can see what materials are going for and give you an estimated cost on Monday."

"Okay," Gayle said, still somewhat baffled by "*It will take as long as it takes*" but willing to go with it for some strange reason. "Thank you."

Kellan walked over to his target board to retrieve the axes.

"No need to walk me out," Gayle said. She could feel his eyes on her as she walked out of the barn. As she approached her car, Muriel came clucking over her way and kicked some dirt at her feet. Gayle grinned down at the funny-looking chicken.

"Not to worry. I'm not on the market. Your man is safe from me."

Muriel gave her a beady side-eye, fluffing up her feathers as Gayle circled around her and got into her car.

Clearly, Muriel wasn't buying it. And Gayle could hardly blame her.

Because, as she drove away, she found herself wishing that she could go back and spend the rest of her day trying to unravel the mystery of Kellan Hayes.

10

NIKKI

Driving through the woods on the way to work, blasting show tunes and singing along at full volume, Nikki felt like she was on top of the world. In spite of the recent snafu with her male boss, life had never been better.

Beth was thriving at college and still texted her nearly every day or called for ten minutes at a time as she walked across campus from one class to another. Nikki loved to hear her daughter chatter about her latest badminton win or what she had learned that day in Introduction to Evolutionary Biology. Spring break was coming up, and they would have lots of time together this summer, too.

Nikki's relationships with her sisters were better than ever. She and Anna talked every week and usually met up for a hike or a meal when Nikki was in Bluebird Bay. Lena was living her best life, running her own business and shacking up with her lifelong best friend and longtime crush, Owen— or, as Anna liked to call him, Lena's Irish Hunk. Gayle was busy rebuilding her life after a messy divorce and the loss of her business, but she had been surprisingly upbeat and hopeful ever since she'd joined her friend Jo in a new business venture. Gayle and Nikki were both working crazy hours and didn't see each other much—even with Gayle sleeping in Beth's room while she looked for a new place to live—but they had stayed up late the night before, chatting and watching a few episodes of some post-apocalyptic show as they ate some of the new recipes Nikki had been testing in order to appease Denis.

Even her long-distance relationship was going well. Sure, she would love to see Mateo more often. Snow days and black ice had kept them from seeing each other as much as they would have liked this winter, but they had been seeing more of each other as the weather cleared. And as busy as she was running her own kitchen in a brand new restaurant, it was just as well that her boyfriend lived two hours away. Most nights, Nikki was too tired after the dinner shift to do anything but go home and sleep. But now that her kitchen staff was well trained, it was easier to get away for a couple of days each week and spend a weeknight at Mateo's house in Bluebird Bay. Not to mention, she used the driving time to record voice memos of recipe ideas for the rest of the year.

It was also lovely that Mateo came down about once a week to have a late dinner at the restaurant and drive Nikki home. All in all, the relaxed nature of their relationship was perfect for right now. Nikki wouldn't have been ready to go all in on romance anyway, not so soon after meeting someone new—even someone as —seemingly— perfect as Mateo. Living in different towns and starting a new, demanding job gave Nikki an excuse for keeping him at arm's length whenever their feelings for each other threatened to pull her along at a quicker pace than she was comfortable with.

Beth had been the center of Nikki's life for eighteen years. Before that, she had let Steve make himself the center of her life. Not once in her adult life had Nikki been fully focused on herself, on *her* goals and dreams. She didn't want to center her life around anyone else. This was *her* time. And just look what she had achieved. Three months in and her recipes were a success; locals loved their food, the reviews — both online and in the local paper— were excellent, and business would be booming once tourists flooded in with the warmer weather that was just around the corner. The kitchen staff at Le Four Locavore was beginning to feel like a real family; Nikki had taken a ragtag team and turned them into a well-oiled machine that rarely made a mistake. Denis had gotten off her back, she and Diane had a great relationship, and she was at the top of her game.

Things were only going to get better from here.

She parked at the restaurant and turned off the car; the silence was startling after blasting Memphis the Musical for a half hour.

Nikki hefted a heavy box from her car and carried it through the restaurant to the kitchen. It was full of strawberry-rhubarb preserves. She had used them to create a phenomenal gastrique earlier in the year, and this week she'd been inspired to create a bright and tangy dressing for their spring salad. Soon enough, there would be fresh rhubarb available. For now, a single jar of preserves in a big batch of dressing could go a long way. She would be sure to preserve the bright red color; it would look amazing over the dark greens and purples of the baby lettuce mix that they used for salad. They could add some sharp cheese if there was enough to spare, or just some local bacon...

God, she *loved* working at a restaurant that focused on local food. The ingredients were phenomenal, and the constantly changing menu was a wonderfully exciting challenge; set menus were such a bore. She had just turned in her mock-ups of spring, summer, and fall menus for that year. They'd change month to month, of course, even week to week, but certain staples could be relied upon. She'd connected with enough local farmers that meat was never an issue, and certain produce would almost always be plentiful at certain times of the year. Starting next month, she would be able to buy fiddleheads, ramps, and even pea greens. After that, May brought all sorts of wonderful fresh foods, most years, anyway. With Maine, it was hard to say anything for sure. Asparagus, fava beans, fresh thyme... Nikki had lived here all her life, and she knew what to expect. She'd been up past midnight every night this week sketching out ideas for this year's menus and testing new recipes. Fresh corn salad in July, apple tarts in August, fried brussels sprouts in October, cranberries galore in November.

She couldn't be more excited to take Le Four Locavore through a full year of seasonal eating.

Nikki took a deep breath as she walked into the kitchen. It was three in the afternoon, and her well-trained staff was hard at work prepping everything that they would need for that night's dinner service. That first breath of the air in a kitchen was always the best, that transition from the fresh spring air outside to the rich scents of roast pork, caramelized apples, simmering red sauce... ambrosia.

Maritza turned and greeted Nikki with a smile. "What've you got, Chef?"

"See for yourself." Nikki set the box down and opened it up.

"Yes!" Maritza crowed. "More gastrique?"

"Nope. I want to use it for salad dressing this time."

"Ay, *que rico*. That's going to be amazing."

"I think so," Nikki agreed cheerfully. Maritza went back to cutting their homemade pasta by hand and Nikki settled in next to her to throw together that night's dressing.

"How are things going with your mom's food truck?" Nikki asked.

"Good! Winter's always slow, but that gives her a chance to rest. Summer makes up for it. We have a big event this weekend, a birthday party down near Portland. Nearly a hundred people."

"That's amazing!" Nikki said. "Good for you. Let me know the next time you guys set up in town. I want some more of that *queso frito*."

"You've got it."

"Hey, Nikki?" Diane stood at the far end of the kitchen, looking sick to her stomach. Nikki frowned, wondering what front-of-house fires their boss was dealing with today.

"What's up?"

"Can I see you in my office, please?"

Nikki's stomach sank. "Sure."

She capped the bottle of vinegar that she was using and followed Diane out of the kitchen. As they walked, Nikki tried to tell herself that everything was fine. Diane was usually stressed about one thing or another; it rarely had any impact on Nikki or her back-of-the-house staff.

So why is she pulling you into her office to talk privately?

Did she want Nikki to cut back on her kitchen staff? They were stretched to the limit as it was. God, what if there had been a call from home? What if something had happened to Beth? But no, that was ridiculous. Nikki's phone was in her pocket; if anything had happened, surely the call would have come straight to her. She resisted the urge to look at her phone and make sure it hadn't died. As she followed Diane into her back office, Nikki felt like she was walking the plank. Her lips felt numb as she sat down. Diane stared down at her own hands for a few seconds that felt like an eternity.

"Did I do something wrong?" Nikki asked quietly.

Diane looked up quickly with a stricken expression. "Absolutely not. You... Nikki, I don't know how to say this, but—" She cut herself off with a low growl. "You know what? No. I'm not doing it. If he wants to be a big man and make the decisions, he can be the one to implement them, too."

"What?" Nikki asked numbly.

"I'm sorry," Diane said. "Just a minute." She stalked to the door and shouted, "Denis!"

Her brother appeared a moment later, looking irritated. When he caught sight of Nikki, his face turned pale —well, pale-*er*.

"You wanted to tell Nikki something?" Diane folded her arms as she glared at him.

"I thought you..." Denis faltered.

"Well, think again. Go ahead. Tell her."

Nikki was starting to feel nauseous.

Denis glared at his sister for a second, then turned to Nikki with a pained smile. "Nicole, you've done such a great job getting us off to a good start here at the restaurant, but I'm afraid we're going to have to let you go. It's nothing against you. You're a great chef. We just... want to move in a different direction. Our cousin Frank is able to come back into the fold, and family is family."

For a long moment, Nikki was too stunned to speak. She just sat and stared. Finally, she said, "So... I'm doing a great job... and you're firing me?"

A red flush crept up the man's neck. "You're welcome to stay on as a line cook. Of course, that would mean firing one of the others, or cutting everyone's hours..."

"A line cook?" Nikki exclaimed. "You want me to make the food I spent countless hours creating under a boss who makes twice as much as me?"

She should stop talking, she knew she should stop talking. A line cook job was still a job, and she had bills to pay. She had a mortgage, she had a daughter to support. But she tasted bile and felt such a burning anger as she turned to Diane and demanded, "You're just going to let him do this?"

Diane bowed her head in shame. "Denis owns more of the business than I do. I tried to talk him out of it, but in the end... it's not up to me."

"Thanks, Didi," Denis said. "Real united front."

"Shut up, Denis," she snapped.

Denis gave her another dirty look and turned back to Nikki. "Look, it's nothing personal. Family comes first, right? Frank and I are like brothers."

"Your *'brother'* left you in a lurch in the middle of opening your restaurant."

Something shifted in Denis's face, a bare twitch in a muscle that gave him away. Nikki's heart dropped, then sped as a realization hit her.

"He didn't leave you in a lurch, did he?" she demanded, reeling with the shock of it. "You brought me in to do the hard part. Create an amazing menu for you, train the staff, and then have him come and run the kitchen on the back of my hard work. You waited for me to create a *year's worth* of menus only to fire me the minute they were done. That is low."

Denis rolled his eyes. "Well, excuse me for giving an untried chef the opportunity to run a restaurant kitchen. I'm sorry it was such a terrible experience for you."

Nikki stared at him for a second before she realized that her jaw was hanging open. She snapped her mouth shut and turned to Diane.

"I didn't know," Diane said quietly. "I had no idea that Frank was coming back. When he was struggling to find local vendors, I thought they both realized that he was out of his depth. He bowed out and Denis told me to find someone new. If I had known—"

Nikki held up her hand, shaking her head. She didn't need to hear any more. She stood and walked out without another word, straight to the kitchen to pack up her knives. In a moment of vindictiveness, she dumped the dressing that she had just made into the trash.

"What's going on?" Maritza exclaimed. Everyone else stopped their work to stare.

"I'm out," Nikki croaked, barely able to speak. She was trembling, physically shaking with anger. Her legs quaked beneath her like she'd just run a marathon, and she felt like she might throw up. Knives, coat... Was that everything?

She had to get out of here.

In a quieter voice, Maritza asked, "You're leaving?"

"Just watch your back with that snake," Nikki said. "He has no integrity." She put her wrapped set of kitchen knives on top of the case of preserves and took a shaky breath.

Maritza shook her head in confusion.

"I'm fired. New chef," Nikki managed to say. "Their cousin."

"What?!" Maritza exclaimed.

Nikki met her gaze and tried to stop the tears threatening to spill over. "It was wonderful working with you. If you ever need a reference, let me know."

She lifted the box and walked through the kitchen, straight to her car. She sat in the driver's seat for a long minute, still trembling from head to toe.

What the hell was she going to do now?

Home was the last place she wanted to be. Lena had enough crap going on. She wasn't ready to face Gayle. Her big sister might not say it much anymore, but she'd surely be thinking *I told you so*.

Nikki was humiliated that she let this happen, that she had let them use her like this. How completely *stupid* to do all that extra work of planning out months of seasonal menus in advance. She should have had some kind of in-depth contract to protect herself, but she had been so excited by the prospect of running her own kitchen that it had never even occurred to her.

She had to get out of here.

Nikki took a deep breath to clear her head, and then

another. She turned her car on and drove down the quiet country road that the restaurant was located on... and found herself turning onto the side of the highway that went *north* rather than south.

She was headed to Bluebird Bay.

She needed to see Mateo.

11

GAYLE

Kellan Hayes had been in every day that week, hard at work on the bar's axe-throwing lanes. Though, as the phrase crossed Gayle's mind, it occurred to her that *hard at work* didn't quite fit; he made it look easy. Some people worked with frequent starts and stops, a flurry of activity followed by a long lull of standing around talking and not doing much of anything at all. That sort of thing infuriated Gayle, particularly when she and Jo were working with a tight budget and needed to open their doors as soon as possible. She watched the young construction workers break off their conversations and pretend busyness when they caught sight of her, and it made Gayle want to hit them over the heads with their own hammers.

Kellan wasn't like that. He worked at a steady pace, stopping only for a meal halfway through his day. Despite the unhurried way in which he moved, his project was coming along much more quickly than anything else they had hired people to accomplish. Gayle had rejected the notion of a chain-link fence as the safety barrier between lanes; rustic was one thing, but chain-link was quite another. It reminded her of batting cages and schools and low-security prisons. No, she'd told Kellan and Jo, that won't work at all. She'd also nixed the idea of solid wood. Too dark, too closed off. They wanted the other patrons to be able to *see* each axe throw, to cheer each other on and wait with excitement for their turn at the game. Kellan's solution was brilliant. Metal field fencing supported by a series of wooden pillars, each one sourced from a young tree trunk or long branch on Kellan's land. The irregular, gnarled, natural look was a perfect fit for the bar, and it was all that you noticed from a distance. The field fencing was strong enough and the gaps small enough to fend off any wide axe throws, but you could hardly see the lines of it until you were standing right there. Kellan was half finished and already the project looked amazing.

Even with the younger workers going in fits and bursts in between their lollygagging, the place was coming along nicely. The whole thing had been an all-consuming whirlwind, but they had gotten so much done. Gayle felt excited to see the finished building—and much more excited to see it filled with a crowd of familiar faces. Many of The Milky Thistle's employees had walked out after Rex and his girlfriend took over, and they were eager to start working for Gayle and Jo again. Even their customers kept pestering them with messages or cornering them in the grocery store to ask when this new bar of theirs would be open. The business that Gayle and Jo had cultivated had little to do with the building or the name of the bar; it was *theirs* in a way that Rex could never take away.

Gayle's phone rang and she pulled it out of the pocket of

her jeans. Reid! Her son didn't call often, and when he did, Gayle was happy to drop what she was doing to answer. She tapped the green circle and Reid's face appeared on the screen.

"Hi, Mom!"

"Hi, Reid! How are you?"

"I'm good. Brittney and I went to a concert on Saturday. It was a blast. It's this local group she likes called Renegade Queen. Not really my thing, but she dragged me along. And they're actually amazing live. It was really fun."

Drawn by the sound of Reid's voice, Jo appeared at Gayle's shoulder.

"Hi, Auntie Jo!" he said when her face came into view.

"Hey, little man," Jo greeted him. Gayle frowned. If *she* ever dared use one of her countless childhood nicknames with her grown children, they would instantly shut down. But somehow, Jo could call twenty-four-year-old Reid by the name she'd started when he was three and his smile didn't falter. Why was that?

"Wait until you see this place," Jo was saying. "We're moving mountains."

The sudden whir of a power drill behind them drowned out the sound of Reid's voice.

"Just a minute," Gayle said as the sound paused and Jo walked away to speak to their contractor. "Let me walk outside."

"How's it going over there?" he asked as she walked down the front steps. "It looks like a construction zone!"

"It is a construction zone." Gayle laughed. "It's going really well. We're on target to open in May."

"I'll be there! I can't wait to see it in person. Just let me know as soon as you have a set date and I'll request the time off work."

"Wow, thank you! I would love it if you could make it out for the grand opening!"

"Of course I'll come, Mom. I wouldn't miss it. I bet Maddy will come, too. She's stressed about work, but all the more reason to get away for a minute in the spring. I'll keep bugging her about it."

"She's stressed with work?" Gayle asked. She could feel her eyebrows coming together, deepening the fine lines on her forehead. It was amazing that she didn't have more, given the stress of raising two teenagers with a philandering husband while running a small business... She supposed there was something to be said for living somewhere that was only warm and sunny for a tiny fraction of the year.

"Who isn't?" Reid said carelessly. "You know Maddy, she's all in on whatever she's doing. She'd stress herself out no matter what her job was. Kind of like you."

"Are you saying that I'm high strung?"

"That's one word for it." Reid was lucky that his smile was so utterly charming. "But hey, that's why I *know* that this bar is going to be a smash success. You work crazy hard and you're brilliant."

"Oh sure," Gayle said, smiling in spite of herself. "Cover your insults with flattery."

"It wasn't an insult, Mom. Just a statement of fact. Speaking of work, though, I should get back to it. I had a bit of time left after lunch so I wanted to call and check in."

"Okay, hon. Thanks for calling. I love you."

"Love you, too, Mom," said Reid as he hung up.

Gayle turned back to the building, wondering what to

tackle next. There were a dozen different things that needed her attention, but her mind wandered stubbornly back towards Maddy and Reid. She should call her daughter tonight and find out what was going on at work. Gayle knew that she shouldn't read too much into her son's casual comment, but she worried about both of them, living so far from home. Not that she *needed* to worry about them. Both of Gayle's children were in steady relationships, both had good jobs, and it seemed that both of them had come to terms with their parents' divorce. She was grateful that she'd had the mental fortitude not to let them see how devastated giving up the bar had made her. Gayle never wanted them to feel torn, as if they had to choose whether to side with their mother or their father.

And they were coming! Probably. Only seeing her children once a year was painful, and they hadn't even come home for Christmas this year. Gayle was happy to give them an excuse to come home for a visit this spring.

Buoyed by the thought of a simultaneous visit from Reid and Maddy, Gayle trotted back up the front steps and into the building. She resisted an urge to go to the far corner of the main room, where Kellan was securing the live-edge posts that he'd brought in to support the field fencing. She found herself intrigued by this quiet, steady man... but she didn't want him to think that she was checking up on him.

Or, worse, that she had a crush.

Still, she couldn't stop wondering what he was doing over there... Gayle found that she was standing motionless at the bottom of the staircase, craning her neck for a glimpse of Kellan. Of all the foolish...

"Earth to Gayle," Jo said.

Gayle blinked and looked over at her friend.

"I have to leave now if I'm going to make my dentist appointment. I might come back if it doesn't take too long, but I'm not sure. If I don't come back by the time the crew leaves, go ahead and lock up. Don't stay too late, okay?"

"You're not the boss of me," Gayle said cheerfully.

Jo chuckled. "Fine, work until midnight. What do I care about? I'll see you tomorrow."

She left and Gayle went upstairs, where she settled down at her desk to get some paperwork done. It took her longer than she thought, and the crew went home for the day as she was finishing up. But Gayle wasn't ready to throw in the towel for the day. It wasn't as if she had anything to go home to. No husband, no children... just her niece's lumpy mattress and a sister who would be at her Locavore restaurant for another four hours, minimum. Gayle sat on the wooden floor, enjoying the quiet as she watched the radiant colors of a Maine sunset over the forest. Then, she flicked on the lights and got to work. She and Jo had chosen a mellow shade of grey for the second floor to cover the dingy white of the walls, and Gayle had all of the supplies that she needed to paint. She played some classical music on her phone and got to work.

It took longer than she thought. It was nine o'clock by the time she finished the detail work in the corners, and her back was killing her. When Gayle tried to stand up straight, she let out a squeak of protest—and then a yelp as a muscle spasmed. The pain faded somewhat and Gayle found herself on her knees. This had happened before, when she was bent in one place too long. Last time it had lasted two days. God damn it. How was she going to drive like this?

She heard the sound of work boots coming up the stairs and let out a sigh of relief.

"Jo? Is that you?"

"'Fraid not," Kellan said, his voice getting closer as he came up the stairs. "But it looks like you could use a little help, there."

Gayle was mortified. She struggled to her feet, but she was still bent over like a crone. Not to mention, covered in splatters of paint and a day's worth of sweat.

"No, thank you. I'm fine." Gayle forced herself to stand up straight, but couldn't keep her face from scrunching with pain as her back spasmed a second time."

Kellan gave her a small, bewildered grin. "Fine, huh?"

Gayle resisted the urge to stick her tongue out at him like a small child.

"You're not fine. Let me help you."

"It's just a little crick," Gayle insisted, edging towards her desk. "It happens. I'll be fine. I just need to walk it off."

Kellan watched her, clearly wondering how that could be possible.

"I can help," he said again. "Turn around."

"What?" Gayle said, baffled. When she didn't comply, Kellan circled around so that he stood behind her.

"Cross your arms over your chest," he commanded gently. "Corpse style, hands on your shoulders."

This time, Gayle did as he said. Mystified, she crossed her arms so that one hand rested on the opposite shoulder of each arm. Kellan stepped up behind her, so close that she could feel his breath on the back of her neck.

"Take a deep breath in."

Gayle inhaled. Just as she reached the top of her breath,

Kellan put his arms over hers. He smelled just as she remembered, forest air and a clean barn. The sheer presence of the man was overwhelming. His chest touched Gayle's back as he squeezed her and lifted her gently, so that her feet barely touched the ground. There was a rapid series of pops as the vertebrae of Gayle's spine clicked back into place. Kellan's arms fell away. The pain was gone. It had taken all of two seconds. Gayle's back was better, but she found herself wanting to lean back and close the space between them, feel his arms around her again. Instead, she stepped away.

She turned to look at him. Kellan was watching her silently, hazel eyes calm and cool.

"Are you a witch doctor or something?" Gayle asked.

Kellan grinned. "No. Just good with my hands."

Gayle tried not to dwell on the implications of that one. "What are you doing here so late?"

"I got here at one today, so staying until nine is just a normal workday. *You*, on the other hand, have been here since early this morning."

Gayle blinked at him in surprise.

"Am I right?" Kellan asked. "What time did you get in?"

"Seven, maybe?"

"Now *that*'s a long day."

"It's normal to work long days at a new business. How do you know what time I got here, anyway?" Gayle asked, trying to keep her voice light. "Are you spying on me?"

"No," Kellan said with a slow smile. "I just know your kind. I *was* your kind."

Gayle didn't like the implication of this. That he had once been foolish as her but had learned the error of her ways. She turned and began to clean up her painting supplies. Kellan just stood here, silently judging. Looking at her as if he had something to say. She smiled wryly as she wondered if that's how her sisters always felt, those times that *she* felt sure that she knew better than they did. She made a mental note to apologize to them —again—, because it was *not* a pleasant feeling. God, was he still just standing there? What was he thinking? Gayle stood and faced him.

"Just say it," she goaded.

Kellan shrugged. "People like you... like I used to be... You can always justify your actions. There's always an argument to be won. I bet when you were younger, people told you that you should be a lawyer."

Gayle tried and failed to hide a grin. She had heard that growing up more times than she could count. She had never *wanted* to be a lawyer. She just wanted to be heard.

"If it's not a new business," Kellan continued, "it's an *old* business that you need to keep rolling. Or there's a project that needs to get done, some new target you have to hit... I just don't subscribe to that anymore."

"What do you subscribe to?"

"Balance."

Gayle looked away. She didn't know many people who had achieved that. What did it even mean, *balance*? For some people, it was an ever-moving target. For others, it was just an excuse to stay in one place.

"Well, good for you," she said carelessly. "You're way ahead of the rest of the world."

"I'm not trying to get ahead of anybody," Kellan said quietly. "That's kind of the point. It's a constant work in progress. First step is at least trying."

He walked over to help her fold a drop cloth she'd been

using, and they cleaned up the rest of Gayle's mess in silence. When they were done, Kellan gave her another of his slow, intoxicating smiles.

"Come up to my place on your next day off," he said. "I'll show you how I like to relax... if you're interested in trying."

Gayle opened her mouth to say no—there were countless reasons not to mix business with pleasure—but found that she couldn't. The truth was, she wanted nothing more than to unravel the inner workings of this man.

"Okay," she said. "You're on."

12

LENA

Gemma enrolled her boys in the local school in early March. Because Cherry Blossom Point was such a small town, there was just a single public school for kindergarten through eighth grade; after that, the kids were bussed to a high school nearby. This meant that Aiden and Liam attended school in the same building; they walked to the bus stop together, rode together, ate lunch together. This was a comfort to both of them, since changing schools for the third time in one year was no small thing.

Lena and Owen didn't hear much from Gemma and the boys that first week. They each checked in with Gemma, who texted back to assure them that everything was fine. The last time they'd seen each other, Lena had given Gemma the number of a grief counselor... but Corinne told her that Gemma had yet to call.

"Everyone grieves on their own time," Corinne had said, "and getting help is a huge step. Anyway, counselors can only help people who are ready to put in the work. Sometimes a person needs to cocoon for a while, first, and that's okay—as long as they're supported and safe."

Owen had invited Gemma and the boys out to dinner more than once, but each time Gemma told him that they were too tired and just needed to eat in. Lena had been tempted to show up with dinner... but she didn't want Gemma to think that she was checking up on the house, or that she didn't trust her. And so a week had passed quickly, Lena and Owen being busy with their own lives. Traffic on Lena's new website had slowed to a crawl after the holiday season, despite her efforts to promote it as a great place to find thoughtful birthday gifts. With Easter around the corner, she was up to her eyeballs in creating local Easter baskets. The baskets themselves were locally made, and they were filled with wonderful gifts. Maple candy, play silks, wooden toys, and even picture books by a local illustrator. Because she couldn't afford for them not to sell, she had made a single sample basket of each option and would be assembling them to order. Owen was busy, too, creating a line of glass vases for a gallery down in Portland.

Finally, on Saturday, they coaxed Gemma into meeting them at Sadie's cafe for a late brunch. Gemma and Liam were quiet as they ate their bagels with lox, but Aiden was full of chatter about his new school. Lena was content to listen to him as she ate a breakfast sandwich filled with cheesy eggs and tomato jam.

"Every time someone reads a book, they get to write the title and the author on a paper leaf and put it on a big tree on the wall that has their name on it. Everyone has their own tree; they go all around the walls of the room. So Miss Prietto made me my own tree and I cut out leaves for every book I've read since September and *guess what?* I have more leaves than anybody in the class! Logan Finch said that I was lying and I hadn't really read them and I said I have too and he was like *prove it* so Miss Prietto asked me questions about the books and I got *all* of them right. If I still have the most leaves at the end of the year, I get a gift certificate for *ten books* at the local book store!"

"That's amazing, Aiden," Lena said. "What a wonderful prize."

"I don't know if I should get new books that the library doesn't have yet or if I should get old books that I already *know* I love, like Harry Potter. I've only read the first three books because Mom says the other ones are too dark, but I could totally read them all. Logan Finch is reading *The Hobbit* and I already read it last year but *he* says that I only have more books than him because I read short little kid books so I got *The Fellowship of the Ring* from the library for reading time. Sometimes I get distracted and I have to read the same page twice, but it's not like it's too difficult for me to read or anything. I'm going to read the whole trilogy and *still* have more books than him."

Owen chuckled. "And do you *like* reading *The Fellowship of the Ring?*"

"It's okay. It's kind of boring, but there are good bits. I liked *The Hobbit* better. At home, I'm reading *Hatchet*, which is way more interesting, even though it doesn't have a bunch of characters."

"Is that... horror?" Lena asked.

"No," Aiden laughed. "It's a survival book! About this kid who's barely older than Liam but when the little plane that he's on crashes and the pilot dies and he's all alone in the forest, he has to survive with nothing but a hatchet. He lives under a rock—kind of like a cave?—and hunts all his own food and stuff. It's so cool."

"Sounds like we should go camping this summer," Owen said.

Liam perked up at that. "Where?"

Owen shrugged. "Wherever you like. I vote for a lake, somewhere we have to hike in."

"My brother Jack does wilderness survival courses in the summertime," Lena said. "He's been talking about doing more stuff for kids, like maybe a camp. Or a week-long camp for families. Learning to build your own shelters and make fire without matches, stuff like that."

"That sounds like the most amazing summer ever," said Aiden with awe.

"It sounds pretty cool," Liam agreed.

"It's a plan," Owen said. "So long as that's alright with you, Gemma?"

"Of course," Gemma said, forcing a smile. "Sounds great."

After brunch, they each got a second drink to go —hot cocoa for Aiden, matcha for Gemma and Liam, and coffee for Lena and Owen— and walked through town to the park. The air was deliciously fresh after a long winter inside, and the day was unseasonably warm for March—well into the fifties. The boys ran into some new friends from school and ended up climbing twenty feet up a tree while the adults sat on a bench watching them. When their friends left, the boys wandered back to finish their now lukewarm drinks.

"Look at that dog," Aiden exclaimed suddenly. They all

turned to regard a Golden Retriever, long hair glinting in the sunlight. "Here dog!"

The dog bounded over. Its whole body wagged in excitement as Aiden tossed his cup and ran to greet it. Liam joined him, his face as bright as Lena had ever seen it.

"He doesn't have any collar, Mom!" Aiden said, wrapping the dog in a protective hug as it licked his face.

Liam looked over at the adults, blue eyes cautious. "We can't just *leave* him here..."

The grownups walked over, and the dog greeted each of them with unadulterated joy.

"Who's the best boy?" Aiden said, ruffling the dog's golden fur. "Who's the goodest dog?"

"We should take him to the vet," Lena said.

"He's not sick," Liam protested.

"No, but he's probably microchipped." Surely a dog this beautiful had someone out looking for him. "The vet will have a reader that can get the owner's contact information."

"They're closed until Monday," Owen said after a quick search on his phone, "and I don't see any sense in driving down to Portland to the animal hospital. I'd take him back to the studio until we find the owners, but it's such a small space... no yard to run around, glass everywhere."

"And we'd have to take him through your workshop every time he needs to pee," Lena agreed. "It's just not feasible."

Owen looked down at the dog with a sigh. "We could take him to the animal shelter."

"No!" Aiden cried, throwing his arms around the retriever's neck.

"The house would work," Lena said hesitantly, looking at Gemma. Owen's sister had hardly said a word all day. A dog would be a companion to her while the boys were at school, but it would be a lot of work, too. She didn't mean to put Gemma on the spot, but surely the boys would ask anyway. "I just mean that I wouldn't mind if you took him back to the house... It's up to you, Gemma."

"Please, Mom," Aiden begged. "I'll walk him every day, I *swear*. Look at him, he *loves* me."

Gemma looked from Aiden to Liam.

"Please?" Liam asked quietly, blue eyes wide.

The dog wriggled free of the boys and chuffed at Gemma's hand. She knelt down on the brown grass and petted the dog. It pressed into her body as close as it could get, and she hugged it, burying her face in its fur.

"What do you think, Gem?" Owen's voice sounded almost normal, but Lena could see the deep worry that hid beneath his cheer. Gemma was a shadow of her old self, and seeing her this way cut him soul-deep. "Think you can keep an eye on this rascal til we find its rightful owner, then?"

Gemma lifted her face up and nodded. Were those tears in her eyes?

"Alright." Owen turned to the boys, who were grinning ecstatically. "Looks like you've got yourself a dog."

The boys whooped and hollered and set to arguing about names.

"He's just a house guest," Owen said belatedly. "You've got to look for his owner."

"But if no one claims him, can we keep him?" Aiden asked. "Can we, Mom?"

Gemma nodded and smiled up at her boys. Her eyes still looked on the verge of tears.

"We should put up Found Dog fliers," said Liam.

"Good man," Owen replied.

"I can go home and print them out." Lena took out her camera and snapped a few photos of the dog as he wound around their feet and nuzzled at their hands.

"Boys, how about you and I go to the pet store? There's one just here in town. We'll need a collar and leash and food, even if he's only staying the night. Gemma, will you stay and watch the wee beast until we get back?"

"Sure," Gemma said, settling back onto the park bench.

"I'll stay with her," Liam told his uncle quietly.

Owen nodded. "Alright, Aiden, that's you and me on a mission. And, go!" He sprinted off across the park and Aiden followed him, laughing with delight.

Liam sat on the bench beside his mother and scratched the dog behind its ears.

"We could name him Diogie," he suggested. "Get it? D - O - G."

Gemma nodded. She was wholly absorbed in petting the dog; it put Lena in mind of the therapy animals that visited trauma survivors. She just hoped that this wasn't a terrible idea... and that they wouldn't get too attached. A gorgeous, social dog like this surely had a family that loved it, and this family had lost too much already.

13

JACK

Corinne gave Jack a smile and a kiss on the cheek as he began unloading the dishwasher. Kiera left early Saturday morning to visit her father, and the house felt quiet without her. Corinne was moving around the kitchen, cleaning up the last of the mess from the night before. She and Kiera had spent the whole evening making chicken soup with dumplings, lemon meringue pie, and chocolate chip cookies. Jack had to admit, he liked having a fridge full of what his sisters liked to refer to as "real food". As if there was something wrong with canned green beans or freeze-dried... okay, he was beginning to see their point. The truth was, there was something soul-nourishing about foods prepared with love right there in his house, something about the smell of simmering broth and the sound of family in the kitchen that turned the house into a *home*. Jack didn't fully understand it, but he sure as hell appreciated it. He didn't know if he could ever go back to his old life, not now. Well, of course he *could*. He could survive it. The point was, he didn't want to.

Jack watched Corinne, admiring the grace of her movements as she went about her work, and he felt tempted to pull her into his arms. But her eyes were far away, still thinking of Kiera. He let her be. What Jack really wanted, as he reflected upon this miraculous transformation of house into home, was for this new family to include his living son. He missed Wyatt.

Dishes safely in the cupboard, Jack wandered over to the dining table. Acting out of habit, he opened his laptop and clicked over to Wyatt's YouTube page. There was a new video, more death-defying ski jumps. Jack's stomach roiled as he watched his boy fly off of a cliff and through the air... Wyatt executed a flawless landing and pumped his fist as bystanders cheered. Jack let out a breath that had caught on his ribcage. It tore his guts up, watching the kid put himself in harm's way. Couldn't he have chosen a safer hobby?

"Why don't you call him?" Corinne asked, and Jack jumped. It wasn't the first time she'd managed to sneak up on him. Not that she was trying to *sneak*—she was just naturally graceful and quiet in the doubled-up wool socks she wore this time of year. She was standing behind him, watching the screen over his shoulder.

Jack grimaced, still looking at the screen. He hadn't told Corinne about the text from Sadie or the fact that his son had changed his phone number just to avoid hearing from him. It was too painful to speak of, and he was deeply ashamed of how badly he'd botched things. First, he had failed River, and then he had failed Wyatt. Corinne had done right by River, and by her second child, too. Kiera adored her mother. How could Corinne possibly understand?

"See what his Easter plans are," Corinne urged softly.

"No time," Jack said. "I have to leave for work in a minute."

Corinne sighed and walked away.

Jack had seen Wyatt only once so far this year, back in January. Wyatt had allowed Jack to drive him to a race... only because Jack was his only option to get there. The entire trip had been strained and awkward, but they had to start somewhere. Jack had thought it was a good start. But ever since, Wyatt had gone to great lengths to avoid speaking to him. It was a punch to the gut.

Jack clicked over to his email to check on new registrations for his summer survival program. There were a few classes running now, mostly for advanced students, but the bulk of the business happened in the summertime. Jack's eyes were drawn to Wyatt's name and to the little green circle that indicated his son was online. Jack took a deep breath and acted on impulse, clicking the icon that would start a video call. He scowled at his own face as it appeared on screen. Surely, Wyatt wouldn't—

"Hey, Dad." Wyatt's face appeared on the screen, bright and grinning. His face was surprisingly dark; Jack could see the faint tan line left by ski goggles. "I never would have thought you knew how to make a video call."

Jack was so surprised to see his son's smiling face that he didn't reply. Lord, but he was grown up.

"Dad? Did the call freeze? Can you hear me?"

"Yeah. Yeah, I can hear you." Jack floundered for a topic. "How's school?"

"School's good. I'm barely passing my French courses, but I'm doing well in German and I'm acing all the classes that are taught in English. We were mostly on the slopes this winter anyway."

"You'll be home soon for Easter, yeah?"

Wyatt's smile faded, and a guarded look came over his eyes. "Yeah."

"Can you make some time for your old man?"

Wyatt shrugged. "I guess we could go to Aunt Gayle's place for burgers, if you want."

"The Milky Thistle's as good as dead," Jack told him. "Rex owns it now."

Wyatt raised his eyebrows. "That sucks."

"She and Jo are working on a new place that will be even better, but it won't be open for a couple months or so." Jack hurried to add, "But we could get burgers somewhere else. Or chowder, Italian. Whatever you want."

"Yeah, sure."

Jack tried to keep the conversation going, turning to the one subject that might keep Wyatt talking. "You said you've been on the slopes a lot?"

"Well, yeah, that's why I'm here." Wyatt's snottiness faded to a grin as he said, "Did you see my new video?"

"Yeah, I did." Just thinking about that dangerous jump made Jack feel sick.

"Awesome, right?"

"Yeah, awesome." Jack's stomach twisted. "Very impressive. Also incredibly dangerous. Shouldn't there be more safety precautions for—"

"I've gotta go." Wyatt's grin had disappeared, replaced by a fierce scowl. "I'll be late for class." He hung up.

Jack sat staring for a moment, feeling utterly defeated. His own stupid face stared back at him, not meeting his eyes. He shut the laptop.

"Jack?" Corinne said as she came down the stairs. "It's nearly eight."

Jack jumped up and began gathering his things.

"I couldn't help overhearing," Corinne said as he grabbed his keys. She walked across the room and ran her hand down Jack's arm. "That sounded like four fifths of a really great conversation. It's a start."

"I messed up," Jack growled. He always did with Wyatt, somehow. Pushed too hard, or not hard enough... never quite right.

"Repairing relationships takes time."

Jack nodded curtly and paused to kiss Corinne on the cheek. "I'll be home for dinner."

The woods were bleak this time of year—no fresh snow, no new color—but Jack liked them all the same. Today especially. They suited his mood. It was a fairly short drive from his house in the woods to the more remote cabin that acted as a central location for their survival school. It was in the opposite direction from town, though, so Jack tried to stagger his schedule this time of year. Some days he went into town to teach self-defense at the academy he'd created, and some days he drove into the woods to teach survival courses. He had good teachers holding down the fort on both ends, so courses ran even on the days he wasn't there.

He arrived before any of his students and went into the cabin for a cup of coffee. Kellan was already there, staring out the window.

Kellan Hayes was the closest thing that Jack had to a

friend. They met up now and again for hunting trips or a day of fishing, the rare times that Jack gave himself a day off work. Jack appreciated a man who didn't feel a need to fill the air with useless words—a man who could be at peace standing in the water for hours on end, just listening to the sound of birdsong and the rustle of branches in the wind. Jack didn't really have friends. He had family, students, and colleagues; Kellan fell into the third category. He'd been teaching classes for the survival academy each summer for five years now, and this year he'd agreed to start in the spring. Demand was increasing each year, and many established students were eager to start earlier in the year and dust off their skills.

"Good morning," Jack greeted him as he poured himself a cup of coffee.

Kellan turned away from the window. "Mornin', Jack. Didn't know you were teaching today."

"Yeah, I've got a novice weekend group. Starting fires, finding north, that sort of thing. You've got the three advanced students coming in, yeah? Same as last weekend?"

Kellan nodded, and a look of amusement crossed his face. "A married couple and a young guy who's set on getting onto Naked and Afraid —— apparently, there's a television show where they drop two people into the woods butt-naked and follow them around with cameras. Anyway, I expected the married couple to be on top of it—they're avid hikers, mountaineers, bow hunters—and the kid to be a pain in the ass. It's the opposite. The couple was bickering with each other all last weekend and contradicting everything I said. Meanwhile, the kid is actually working really hard. Picking stuff up real quick."

"I guess Naked, Afraid, and Starving would be one too many adjectives."

Kellan grinned. "How are things with you?"

"Great," Jack said reflexively. It was mostly true. "Corinne's settled in, starting to establish a practice in Cherry Blossom Point. And the academy is good. Business is booming."

"And Wyatt?" Kellan and Wyatt had never met, but Jack had talked about him before.

"I talked to him today..." Jack trailed off, running a hand over his short, bristly hair. "I think I stepped in it. He was all excited about this ski jump and—honestly, it scares the crap out of me, seeing him risk his neck like that. So I was stupid, I got on his case instead of just smiling and nodding like I should have done."

"That'll do it," Kellan said. "Boys that age, almost men... they have a hard time listening to their daddies. Probably he feels a little like you gave up the right to give him that kind of grief."

"So I'm just supposed to let him put himself in harm's way and not say anything at all about it?" Easier said than done.

Kellan shrugged. "If it was me, maybe I'd spend some time mending fences before I started drilling holes in them again." A car pulled in out front and Kellan said, "That's my crew. Good luck with your newbies today, Jack."

He walked out and Jack stood at the window for a while, sipping his bitter black coffee. The evergreens beyond the window were dark, and Jack's face stared back at him. It seemed he couldn't escape his own reflection today. Kellan was right. It was more or less the same thing that Jack's grief counselor had been saying.

"The goal of counseling," he'd told Jack earlier that week, "is ultimately to help you change your outlook on things. Once that happens, you can begin to reverse some of the negative effects that your previous understanding and the resulting choices have had on your life and the lives of those around you."

Jack had begun to realize that, in his attempts to keep his loved ones safe, he had become so rigid and controlling that he had actually pushed them away. He'd been working on that—it helped that Corinne would accept nothing less than full autonomy over her life, even now that they were living under the same roof—but working to change his future behavior wasn't enough. He needed to make more of an effort to make up for the past... especially with Wyatt.

14

GAYLE

Gayle found that she loved rising at first light and getting a jump on the day. For years, she had been a night owl out of necessity, staying late at The Milky Thistle and catching up on sleep the next day, rising around nine or so to do it all over again. It had taken her a while to adjust, and she had been surprised to realize that she much preferred early mornings to late nights.

Would she be able to continue this once the restaurant opened, or would she have to stay late each night as she had all those years at the bar? Gayle heard Kellan's voice in her head, his calm advice on finding balance. Surely, she could let Jo or a general manager handle the late nights? Lord knew there would be enough else to do, between the dinner service and events and talks of weekend brunch. She should find some time to sit down with Jo and discuss the running of the place; Gayle had someone in mind for general manager, a server who had taken on more and more responsibilities at The Milky Thistle over the years. She knew Jo would agree.

A FRESH START

Gayle showed up at Sadie's cafe a good ten minutes before they were officially open, but Sadie greeted her with a smile. Gayle felt a new wave of gratitude that Jack's ex-wife had been so consistently kind to all of them, even following their divorce. She had never made them feel uncomfortable coming into her café, and had certainly never tried to keep Wyatt from seeing Jack's side of the family. No, that breech was entirely Jack's fault... and maybe a little bit Gayle's fault, too, she admitted to herself. Wyatt and Lena were plenty close, and he'd always been tight with Beth and Nikki... but for years, Gayle had hardly seen him at all. He'd given her the cold shoulder ever since he'd hit the double digits, and Gayle had quickly given up. Not that she ever made a conscious decision to cut ties with her brother's son... she had just been too wrapped up in her own life to worry about him... especially after he'd left for boarding school. A faint spasm of guilt moved in Gayle's chest as she thought of how her carelessness might have contributed to this rift in her family and in the heart of her twin brother... it caused no small amount of grief to their father, and surely it had hurt the boy in ways she didn't understand. Maybe she could get everyone together for Easter, when Wyatt came to visit. Sadie, too, of course. She was still family, and Gayle had seen her and Corinne being cordial to each other last year—no hard feelings there. Gayle would ask Beth to help her convince Wyatt to spend Easter with the family; the girl could be persistent when she wanted to be. Comforted by this plan of action, Gayle greeted Sadie with a smile.

"How are you, Sadie?"

"I'm well." Sadie was a small, dark-haired woman—somewhat care-worn, but still a handsome woman. And quite possibly the kindest soul in town, not to mention a competent businesswoman.

Where is Sadie's Kellan Hayes? Gayle wondered suddenly, and immediately tossed the absurd non sequitur from her mind.

"Wyatt comes home soon," Sadie continued. "I can't wait to see him."

"I was just thinking about Wyatt. I miss him, we all do. I wonder if we could all spend Easter together, or just a family dinner while he's in town?"

A shadow passed over Sadie's face, but her smile held. "That sounds lovely. I'll ask him. What can I get for you today, Gayle?"

"Three of those amazing orange-peel chais of yours," Gayle said. "To go, please. And three of your Mediterranean bagels." They were phenomenal. Fluffy scrambled eggs with luscious feta and a house-made pesto. She just hoped they would travel well; she'd promised Jo breakfast today. Gayle often forgot to eat, and Jo had forced her to pause for breakfast most days this week. Gayle owed her one. Well, Gayle owed her a few, but a decadent bagel and chai was a good start.

"Which kinds of bagels would you like?" Sadie was a phenomenal baker, and even her bagels were made in house. The *real* way, boiled first. Gayle scanned the flavors for the day.

"Garlic and onion, definitely." Bad breath be damned. They were delicious.

Gayle paid, Sadie wrapped up her order, and she was on her way. She studiously avoided looking at The Milky Thistle as she drove by. The wound Rex had dealt her was healing, but it still hurt. Honestly, it hurt a lot. She nearly passed it without looking, but a strange flash of color caught her eye. Gayle glanced up and saw that they had replaced her beautiful handmade wooden sign with some awful neon eyesore. She wanted to punch something, but she settled for turning a classic rock station on full blast and shouting along to snatches of the chorus of each song as she drove to work.

Jo and Lena were already there, chatting as they pulled boxes from the trunk of Lena's car. Jo's aged pit bull stood nearby, wagging its tail as it sniffed and snuffed the ground. Gayle pushed thoughts of The Milky Thistle out of her head and exited her own car with a flourish, holding up the bags marked *Sadie's*.

"I come bearing bagels!" she announced. Lena snatched at the bags with a grin, and Gayle ducked back into the car for their drinks. They carried everything upstairs, where some of the boxes that Lena had brought were waiting for them. The first round of specially made tables and chairs had been delivered the day before, and they were gorgeous. A perfect fit for the space, just as Gayle had hoped. The three women sat down at one of the new wooden tables and looked over Lena's samples as they ate. There were copper mugs, pewter tankards, and handmade ceramic mugs—all made by local artisans. Owen had contributed a few different samples, heavy glasses in different shapes and sizes. Gayle and Jo had considered going with mass produced, mainstream items like most restaurants did... but their instincts told them that standing out by investing in unique offerings by locals would lead to better business in the long run. Gayle was still considering lightweight, mass-produced items for their servers' trips up and down the stairs... but for the lower level that would hold the bar, and even for special cocktails going up and down the stairs, she wanted something unique.

"Now, this one," Jo said heartily as she pulled a tankard from the box, "this one is the ticket. I feel like a Viking just holding it."

Gayle laughed. "Is that the vibe we're going for, then?"

"Um, hello? We have people throwing axes downstairs. It already feels like a Viking hall."

"Been to a lot of Viking halls, have you?"

"Nah, just staying up late watching *The Last Kingdom*." Jo turned to Lena. "What do you have that's wood? I'm thinking some tree trunk slice kind of platters for Gayle's fancy appetizer trays, or even old-school wooden trenchers."

"I didn't bring anything today, but I know the perfect person." Lena pulled out her phone and clicked through the pages of her website. "Look here."

Jo took the phone and squinted at the screen. "Yes, perfect. Take a look, Gayle."

"Oh, that oval one is gorgeous," Gayle said as she scrolled through the woman's offerings. "And yeah, this trencher could be good for crudité platters in the summertime."

"Okay, now, check out these dishes," Lena said, pulling a short stack of ceramic plates from a box. "These are the three colors I thought would work with your decor."

One option was a lovely, deep espresso. Another was a reddish mahogany that Gayle didn't care for. The third was a pleasant mocha color. The first one was her favorite, but she suspected that the third would be better as a backdrop for the sort of food they would be serving here. Meat on a dark brown plate didn't sound appetizing. Still, it was a lovely color, and they were sure to have creamy white potatoes or bright orange carrots all around the meat...

"It's hard to decide without seeing them full of food," Jo said.

"Yeah, I was thinking the same thing," Gayle agreed.

Lena grabbed the uneaten half of Gayle's bagel and destroyed it, splitting it between the three plates.

"That was going to be my lunch," Gayle said in dismay.

Lena ignored her. She stood up and whisked all three plates away, then came back holding just the espresso-colored option. She set it down with a flourish, saying, "Your brunch, good sir."

Gayle glared at her, still frustrated with how Lena had massacred a perfectly good bagel. "We won't be serving bagels here. It's not the same."

"Hey, Steve!" Jo called over a carpenter who was working on the banister of the stairs. When he reached the table, Jo gestured to the plates and asked, "Which one do you like best."

He shrugged, looking bewildered. "They're all brown."

Gayle and Lena groaned in unison as Jo regarded the man with narrowed eyes. "Would you say that about different colors of wood? Meh, mahogany, birch... What does it matter? They're all brown."

"But... they're just plates."

Jo sighed. "Get out of here, Steve."

There was another set of footsteps on the stairs, and Gayle's heart fluttered as Kellan Hayes came into view. He was wearing his usual uniform of brown work pants and a worn plaid shirt. Gayle had never much liked that lumberjack look, but on *Kellan*...

"Sorry to disturb you ladies, but I'm about to start work and I wanted to show you something." He laid an axe on the table, one of the undersized, lightweight varieties meant for throwing. The head was dark, nearly black, and the handle was some sort of lightweight wood. "Most of the throwing axes that you can buy commercially have aluminum handles, if not plastic, and the metal is shiny as a silver wedding band. This guy has high-carbon steel and local wood. A buddy of mine makes them. I thought they'd be a better fit for Hunter's Gathering than some commercial stuff."

Jo picked it up, testing the weight and balance. "I like it. Just need to test it out downstairs, soon as you're ready."

"I'm ready. The first lane's done." Kellan set a business card on the table. "Here's my buddy's name and number. He wrote some quotes on the back and dates, depending on how many you'd need."

"Thanks," Jo said. "I'll be down to test it out in a minute."

"No rush." Kellan turned to go.

"Hey, Kellan," Gayle said, her voice reaching out to pull him back like an arm on his shoulder. "What do you think of these plates?"

Kellan turned to regard the three plates that Lena had dirtied with scraps of bagel. "What about them?"

"We're trying to choose a color for the restaurant."

He looked at the plates for a long moment, then touched one broad finger to the lightest option.

"With game, the meat is often served with jus, or darker sauces and berries. I think the mocha will make those pop more." He held Gayle's eyes for a second, then nodded and turned to go. She could hear him whistling on his way down the stairs.

A FRESH START

Lena fanned herself dramatically. "I love my clean-shaven Irishman, but that man has a way about him, doesn't he?"

"A real man," Jo said. "They're in short supply these days."

Gayle's mouth was glued shut. She was afraid to open it in case she drooled.

Nope. No. Bad bad bad.

She should *not* be thinking about their contractor that way. They were colleagues... friendly colleagues, but that was all. Still, she *did* sort of promise him that she would let him teach her to relax, and her next day off was in a couple days. She would text him later to firm up their plans.

Just as friends.

Just as an experiment...

15

NIKKI

Nikki sat on Mateo's comfortable oversized sofa, staring into the fire he had started that morning while she was still in bed. Mateo walked in from the kitchen and handed Nikki a cup of coffee.

"Cream and a dash of maple syrup," he said as he sat down next to her. "Just how you like it."

"Thank you." Nikki gave him a smile, but it fell quickly from her face. Her whole being felt too heavy to maintain it, to do much of anything at all.

"Are things looking any brighter after a good night's sleep?" Mateo asked. He didn't sound particularly hopeful that she would have a positive answer for him.

Nikki took a long sip of the rich, hot coffee. She couldn't bring herself to look at him, so she found herself staring into the hearth again. It was nothing against Mateo; she just felt like hibernating for a month or so. Not that taking that much time off of work was a feasible option... her time in Bluebird Bay the year before had eroded her savings, and what Nikki had left was set aside for her daughter. Beth's tuition was being paid for by a scholarship, but she still needed Nikki's help with rent, books, food... Nikki needed to find a new job —a good one—and fast. She took another gulp of coffee.

"I knew there were no guarantees with this job," she told Mateo. "You never know how long a new restaurant will stay open. But God, I thought I had a year, at least. I felt so hopeful that this place would make it. I was so excited about creating new menus." Tears of disappointment stung Nikki's eyes and she blinked angrily, refusing to let them spill over. "I did so much work for them that I didn't even get paid for! Finding vendors, building relationships with local farmers, recipe testing... I did all the hard work of learning how to make the most of a brand new kitchen and training an entire staff from scratch —and then, just when we'd hit our stride, I'm out on my ass."

"It's just as well," Mateo said. "You don't want to keep working for people who would treat their employees that way."

"I do, though. I loved that kitchen. I loved my staff. I had such plans." She took a long, shaky breath. It was all so unfair. But spiraling wouldn't do her any good. With high drama, she said, "For one brief and shining moment, I ran my own kitchen in a phenomenal restaurant."

"And you will again," Mateo assured her. "You'll find something better."

Nikki let out a grim chuckle. "Not likely. I can't wait around for something like that to open up again. I'm going to have to take the first decent job I can find if I want to pay my mortgage *and* Beth's rent."

Slowly, Mateo asked, "What if you looked for something in Bluebird Bay?"

Nikki looked at him sharply. His expression was so sweet and hopeful that it gave Nikki a jumpy, uncomfortable feeling. It was a heavy thing, to be the object of another person's hopes and dreams.

"You wouldn't even have to find something right away," he told her. "You could wait for the perfect job to open up. I have a great job here managing our family properties, and since you don't have a job holding you in Cherry Blossom Point... you could rent out your house and let me take care of you until you found a fantastic job in Bluebird Bay. It would take away the stress of needing to find something right away, and we could be together."

"I don't know, Mateo..."

"I've been thinking about asking you anyway. I miss you, Nikki. This long-distance thing is hard. It's just not enough for me anymore. We've hardly seen each other in months."

Whatever Nikki had expected when she'd driven up to Bluebird Bay, it wasn't this. She had only known Mateo for... what, five months? She didn't feel ready to leave Cherry Blossom Point, her family, her *home*. It wasn't as if they lived on opposite sides of the country. They could see each other every week if she was going to be working as a line cook instead of a head chef.

"I'll have more time to spare now that I'm not running my own kitchen," she said. "I can drive up every weekend... or whatever my days off end up being."

"I'd rather see you every night," Mateo told her with quiet insistence. "If you don't want to move here, I could move in with you. At some point. Just... think about it?"

"I will." Nikki glanced at her watch. Not strictly time to leave for the diner, but close enough. She drained the last of her coffee. "I need to leave. I'm meeting Anna for breakfast. I'll be back soon and we can go for that hike, yeah?"

"Sure." Mateo's smile was dim. "And maybe the bowling alley for dinner?"

Nikki smiled at the thought of the sweet old lady in the kitchen behind the bowling alley. Best chowder in Bluebird Bay, hands down.

"Deal," she said.

Anna wasn't at the diner yet, but another familiar voice greeted Nikki the moment she walked through the door.

"Nikki! What a wonderful surprise! It's been too long!" Eva set her tray down on the nearest table, ignoring the baffled looks of the customers who were sitting there, and nearly tackled Nikki with a fierce hug.

"Hi, Eva." Nikki laughed, returning the woman's hug. Not for the first time, she prayed that God give her even half of the energy that Eva had when she reached that age. Long past the age at which most people retired, Eva hadn't slowed down a bit. She was still in motion now, steering Nikki towards her favorite booth. Eva picked up her tray in passing, set things down at their proper table with a greeting and a smile, and then turned back to Nikki as she slid into the booth.

"What brings you to town? Where's Mateo?"

"I just came from his place. I'm meeting Anna for breakfast."

"Oh good, two of my favorite faces!" Eva reached out to touch Nikki's cheek. "You seem not quite yourself. What's wrong?"

"The restaurant that I was working for fired me," Nikki admitted.

"Of all the... complete and utter fools. Why? Where are they going to find someone with half your talent?"

"From their aunt's uterus. By way of France."

Eva stared in incomprehension for a second before what Nikki had said clicked, and she chuckled.

"Nepotism," she said darkly. "What's a girl to do?"

"Waitress!" A shrill-voiced woman waved at Eva, her face set in a scowl.

Eva grinned at Nikki and rolled her eyes. "What can I get for you?"

"Some herbal tea, maybe?" Coffee on an empty stomach had only exacerbated the anxiety that was strumming Nikki's nerves, but she didn't have much of an appetite.

"And to eat?" Eva persisted.

"Fruit salad?" Nikki suggested weakly.

Eva gave her a narrow look and a *hmph* of disapproval as the same woman shouted, "*Excuse* me!"

"I'll find something for you," Eva promised Nikki as she walked away. A few minutes later, she returned with mint tea and some sort of cobbler topped with a scoop of ice cream.

"Plenty of fruit in there," she said with satisfaction, already walking to the next table over.

Nikki chuckled and took a tentative bite of the cobbler. It was divine. Berries and stone fruit and ginger. She was so focused on the warm fruit and creamy vanilla ice cream that she didn't even notice when Anna walked in... until she slid into the booth next to Nikki and gave her a spine-popping hug.

"It's so good to see you!" Anna retreated from Nikki's bench and slid in across the table.

"You too," Nikki said, trying to muster up some enthusiasm. It *was* good to see her sister—after spending most of their lives in complete ignorance that the other existed, it felt like she could never get enough time with Anna to make up for all the time that they'd lost—but it was hard to muster up the proper enthusiasm for everything today.

"You seem sluggish," Anna said with a suspicious look at Nikki's tea. "Did you kick coffee?"

"I already had one cup," Nikki said with a laugh.

"Did you already have breakfast, too, or did you skip straight to dessert?"

"The latter."

"I approve. Eva, angel of mercy," Anna said as the waitress approached their table, "I am starving. Would you please bring me an omelet and also a bowl of whatever that divine mess is that Nikki's eating?"

"Which omelet would you like?"

"I don't care, so long as it's hot and stuffed with food."

"You've got it."

"And coffee!" Anna called after her. "All of the coffee!"

Nikki grinned at her sister. Just being around her was a good pick me up. "Are you sure you need it?"

"What do you think keeps me so witty and delightful?" Anna asked.

"Your sparkling personality?" Nikki asked sardonically.

"I suppose you can credit my wit there, but it can get rather dark without proper caffeination. And slow... is it still wit if it's slow? I don't believe it is."

"You seem particularly chipper today." Nikki and her

half-sister looked so much alike that people occasionally mistook one for the other. Looking at Anna was like looking at a particularly hopeful vision of her future... what Nikki would look like in ten years if the next decade of her life was phenomenally successful... and sunny. Anna was a lovely shade of golden after a trip to Hawaii with Beckett.

Anna shrugged happily. "Life is good. I was feeling a little twitchy after staying home all winter, so booking that gig in Hawaii was just the ticket. Beckett and I made a vacation out of it. He trudged through the jungle like a trooper with me and picked up about a thousand mosquito bites while I photographed endemic birds. But we made time for vacation stuff, too. Black sand beaches, waterfalls. We even went night snorkeling with giant manta rays. Big as a boat, Nikki, I kid you not."

"That sounds amazing."

"It was pure magic. But what really surprised me was how happy I was to be *home*. Teddy's growing so fast that we hate to be away from him for long. I swear he learned fifty new words in the ten days we were gone. One trip a year is Beckett's speed, and I might be okay with that these days. Though that's Hawaii twice in a row... if I can't entice him to get a passport and go somewhere more interesting next time, I might need to take a second trip each year. Want to come to Thailand?"

Nikki thought immediately of all of the phenomenal foods that she could learn to cook if she actually made time in her life for travel. "I would love that."

"Let's do it! I love my life here, but I wouldn't feel quite myself if I never left the country again."

"I've never left the country at all." Nikki had traveled a bit, but all within the continental U.S.

"Sisters trip! Or you, me, and Beth this summer if she can get away. We have to do something, even if it's no more than a few days on a lake somewhere. Do you think Lena and Gayle would be interested?"

"I don't know. Maybe."

Eva brought Anna's food, and the torrential chatter slowed as she ate an omelet overflowing with vegetables, bacon, and cheese.

"What about you?" she asked Nikki. "How are you and Mateo? How's Beth?"

"Beth is good. She's happy at school. Things with Mateo are good, I guess. He wants me to move in with him."

"Wow! And how do you feel about that?"

"I don't know. I think it's just so soon, we've only known each other for..." Well, about as long as she and Anna had known each other. "We just met in the fall. He's amazing, but I don't feel ready to uproot my whole life just to move in with him."

"Yeah, I get that." Anna grinned. "You only uproot your life for long-lost sisters."

"I didn't uproot my life to come here," she shot back with a grin. "I just put it on pause."

"Fair enough. He expects you to leave an amazing new job? That really surprises me. He was so excited for you!"

"Well, yeah, about that..." Nikki sighed, poking at her congealed cobbler and melted ice cream. "They fired me."

"What?!" Anna exclaimed. "Why?"

"To hire their cousin. They didn't technically fire me, I guess. They offered me a lesser position for lower pay. I didn't want to keep working there. Not after the way I was treated. But it means I don't even get unemployment, and I need to find something else quick. I probably should have stayed on as a line cook in the meantime."

"Nah, forget them. You'll find something. The question is, are you going to look here or in Cherry Blossom Point? Why not look for jobs in both places and see what happens?"

"I guess that would make sense," Nikki said dully. She didn't like the idea of her job prospects deciding where she was going to live; she wanted more control over her life than that.

"You know what the Sullivan women do when we're faced with difficult decisions? We make lists!"

"Lists," Nikki repeated skeptically.

"Yep!" Anna pulled a used envelope from her purse and fished out a pen. "You dictate."

Nikki smiled at Anna's calm assurance that everything could be solved with a pros and cons list. "Well, I would love to see you more often. And I would like to see more of Mateo, too, but not necessarily if it meant moving in with him? I mean, seeing more of him is a pro, but..."

"Cons," Anna said, "giving up your house. What else?"

"I would miss Lena so much, even Jack a little... and I hate to leave town when Gayle is still reeling from her divorce. She hasn't even found a place to live yet; she's been sleeping in Beth's room. Though I guess she could have my house," she murmured, thinking out loud. "Not that she'd want it."

"What else?" Anna encouraged her.

"I can't leave Dad." As Nikki said this aloud, she realized that this was the reason that underpinned all the others. "I would miss him like crazy, but more than that, I feel a sense of responsibility. He's nearly eighty years old. I hate the idea of moving away just when he needs me most. I know that sounds ridiculous when he has three other kids in town…"

"That's not ridiculous," Anna said. "Family comes first."

"As much as I would love to see more of you and Mateo… I don't know how many years we have left with my dad. I can't move away. Not right now."

Anna smiled at her and crumpled the scrap paper. "You didn't need a list after all."

"But I did need to talk it through. Thank you. I'll just have to find a job in Cherry Blossom Point."

"You will," Anna said with confidence. The conversation moved on to lighter things as they finished their food, working together to eat Anna's overstuffed omelet. Anna told her about the weekly events that her niece Max was hosting at her bookshop. Slam poetry on Tuesdays and music on Fridays, usually featuring her cousin's girlfriend Alice on the fiddle. They laughed over stories of Beckett's grandson Teddy and of Beth when she was that young. Nikki's worries eased as she sat with her sister… but as she drove to Mateo's house, anxiety began to weigh on her again.

She wasn't ready to move here, and she couldn't let Mateo uproot his life to move to Cherry Blossom Point. Not yet, at least. They'd have to keep up with a long-distance relationship.

The question was, would he even want to?

16

GAYLE

Gayle felt increasingly frustrated as she sorted through her clothes. Like her life, her wardrobe was a hot mess. Some things she had hung in the closet next to her niece's forgotten sweaters and senior prom dress. Some fit in the dresser. But most of her clothes were packed in boxes or sprawling out of a suitcase. She could not find her favorite sweater, and anyway—she had no idea *what* to wear for "relaxing" with Kellan Hayes. Gayle had texted him yesterday to ask for a hint at what sort of clothes and shoes she would need... and nothing.

He'd never replied.

Was he ghosting her or what? Normally, if someone ignored Gayle when she contacted them to confirm an appointment, she would assume that they'd flaked. She was tempted to stay home today rather than going to Kellan's cabin in the woods. And yet... she was drawn to him, to a degree that she tried unsuccessfully to deny.

Eventually, she settled on comfortable jeans, hiking boots, a lightweight shirt made of soft merino wool, and her second-favorite sweater. She set her radio to the classical music station as she drove, but it did nothing to soothe her nerves. What if she got there and Kellan was nowhere to be found? Would his dog attack her if she walked up when his master was away?

She needn't have worried. Kellan was sitting on his front porch when she arrived, swaying on a porch swing like an old man. A very *fit* old man, Gayle admitted to herself. Instead of his usual plaid collared shirt, Kellan sat out in the frigid morning air with nothing over his arms but a single thin layer of wool, much like the shirt that Gayle wore beneath her sweater and coat. She could see his muscles clearly beneath the thin fabric. Not the grotesquely oversized muscles of a man who spent his days indoors lifting weights, but the balanced musculature of a man who spent his days doing *real* work, moving steadily from one task to another. She felt certain that Kellan had built the bench he was sitting on himself. It hung from the rafters on four oversized chains.

"Am I late?" Gayle asked as she walked up the path to his house. She felt a prickle of irritation as she remembered the unanswered text message and asked, "Were you waiting on me or did you forget that I was coming?"

"None of the above." Kellan gave her a bemused, subtle smile. His gaze was steady, and yet Gayle couldn't shake the impression that he was looking her up and down. "I was just sitting."

"I didn't know if we were still on for today," Gayle said.

"Why's that?"

"I texted you. You never replied."

Kellan's smile broadened. He stood, walked into his house, and reappeared a moment later. He tossed something underhand, and Gayle caught it reflexively. It was a sleek black rectangle with numbers on one side, like a calculator.

"JustaPhone," Kellan said. "That's what they call it, the company. Holds a charge for nearly a month. No text, no internet, no dings and pings. Just a phone. I don't get text messages."

Gayle blinked down at the strange little device. "Oh."

"You're welcome to call me next time." Kellan walked down his front steps and accepted the phone when Gayle held it out to him. "Have you ever been fly fishing?"

Gayle shook her head.

"You live in Maine and you've never been fly fishing?"

"Guilty as charged," she replied with a nervous smile.

As before, she felt overwhelmed by Kellan's presence when he came this close to her. She felt an absurd urge to close the space between them and run her fingers over the subtle lines of the muscles that she could see beneath his shirt... It was an utterly foreign impulse, and quite frankly, it was terrifying. She had been attracted to other men, of course. Rex had been very handsome when he was young, and there had been a few others who had caught her eye over the years. But good lord, never like this. The man was magnetic. And Gayle still had no idea if he was interested in her *like that*. Sure, he'd invited her back to his house a second time. But he had invited her brother, Jack, up to his cabin multiple times, as well. This magnetic pull that Gayle felt might be entirely one-sided. Only...

You smell good. Gayle could still hear the bewildering non sequitur that he'd spoken so casually the last time she was here. Surely, he wouldn't say something like that to *Jack*? Oh hell, maybe he would. He'd said it so casually...

You smell good, Jack, old buddy! Do you make your own soap like I do? What's your recipe?

Pull yourself together, Gayle.

"You should know where your food comes from." There was no reproach in his tone. Kellan spoke as if this were a simple statement of fact. "Come on in, and we'll get you outfitted."

Kellan offered her a warmer coat to replace the one she had brought and donned one himself. They each pulled a pair of rubber waders over their jeans and hiked out to a small lake just down the hill from Kellan's cabin.

Despite her initial trepidation, by the time they started, she was actually kind of excited. An hour later, though?

Not so much.

The whole thing felt like a lesson in futility. Even when Gayle started to get the hang of the motion, it didn't matter. They didn't catch anything all morning—not even Kellan, not even a nibble. There were a million other things that she could be doing right now besides standing in the muck of a lake, staring at her own wavering reflection in the surface of the water as she tried to trick a fish into thinking her lure was a bug when she could just *buy* whatever sort of fish she damn well pleased.

When she glanced over at Kellan, he was smiling at her in amusement.

"What?" she snapped.

Kellan shrugged and whipped his line again, tapping the surface of the water with his fly. "You're cute when you're frustrated."

Gayle felt a blush color her cheeks. "Why aren't *you* frustrated? You haven't caught a thing."

"It's a little early in the year for fishing," Kellan said placidly. "April's better, or May. Some years this lake is still frozen in March. But I usually catch *something* just after the thaw, if I stay long enough. Anyway, it doesn't much matter if I don't. Catching a fish is just the icing on the cake."

She heaved a small, quick sigh of frustration. "What's the cake, then?"

Kellan grinned and made a sweeping gesture with one broad hand. Gayle looked up, really *seeing* the scene in front of her for the first time. It was a gorgeous day, the dark evergreens and bare deciduous trees stark against the blue, blue sky. The air was crisp and clean and perfect. They could see clear across the lake to the unbroken forest on the other side.

She had been so caught up in what she was trying to do, so frustrated with herself for not immediately mastering a new skill, that she'd barely even looked around. She'd been worrying about if she was going to be any good at fly fishing, about what Kellan was thinking or what she could be accomplishing this morning if she had gone into work instead... Her mind had been flitting from one thing to another, anywhere but *here*. The breathtaking scene right in front of her. She could feel her heart rate slow as she settled into her body and this present moment in time. As the day went on and the sun shone warm on Gayle's face through the chill spring air, she found herself lulled into a sort of meditative state. Her breathing was slow and deep, and she felt relaxed in a way that she couldn't remember feeling in a long, long time.

And when she caught her first fish? She was almost giddy with excitement.

"Great job! Look at you," Kellan said, a wide grin splitting his face.

From then on, she was...hooked.

"Let's catch some more. I think I'm really getting it now!"

Hours later, as Kellan loosed the hook from fish number five, she felt a sense of accomplishment she'd only known at work.

"That'll be enough for dinner and some for the freezer as well," Kellan said with a satisfied nod. "We should start back up the hill before we lose the light."

Gayle was shocked to see that the sun was nearly brushing the tops of the trees to the west. How had she spent an entire day just standing in a lake? It felt like it had gone by in a blink.

They walked back up to the cabin, Kellan carrying the fish, and left their sloggers and heavy coats on the back porch. Gayle thanked him for a wonderful day and began to put on her own coat, and he gave her a look of surprise.

"You did all this work. Now to enjoy the spoils. You'll stay for dinner, won't you?"

A warm smile spread across Gayle's face, and she dropped her coat. "Sure."

Kellan stoked the fire that he'd banked in his wood-burning stove, then showed Gayle how to scale a fish with the back of a kitchen knife, gut it, and filet it.

"What are you doing?" he asked as Gayle picked up the cutting board full of fish guts and carried it towards the trash.

"Cleaning up as we go?" Gayle's voice trailed off, unsure of what she'd done wrong.

"Don't you dare. That's good food."

She set the platter of entrails down on the counter. "You can't be serious."

Kellan grinned. "Not for us. For my girls. Muriel loves fish guts."

Gayle wrinkled her nose. "I thought chickens were vegetarians."

"No." Kellan laughed. "They'll take bugs over grain any day. You should see Muriel hunt down a mouse. They're dinosaurs, just a bunch of fluffy little velociraptors. The guts are good for them. I have a few barn cats, too. I don't feed them much, but the occasional feast keeps them friendly."

"But... the cage-free eggs at the store say vegetarian fed."

"Those poor girls," Kellan said. "All cooped up in one building eating wheat all day. Same with people, I guess. Most of them sign up for a life that's more or less the same. Outside five minutes a day or so on cement and right back in again. Never could wrap my mind around how so many people incarcerate themselves voluntarily, one day after another. Chained to a desk."

Gayle stared at him, dumbstruck. Had he just said something profound, or was it just that his deep, steady voice was utterly mesmerizing? She honestly had no idea. The early days with Rex had been like that; his movie-star looks and charm had convinced her that he was much cleverer than he really was. The fog of physical attraction made it hard to see people clearly for who they were. Is that what was happening here?

Kellan Hayes was no movie star. He wasn't unattractive, but neither was he the sort of man who turned heads walking down the street. And yet... the attraction that Gayle felt for this man was stronger than anything that she had felt for the more classically good-looking men who had pursued her all throughout her youth. He was so easy in his own skin. So sure, and confident, but not cocky.

It was a heady elixir.

Gayle ran her hands beneath the frigid water of the kitchen sink and splashed some on her face. Kellan put a blob of something white in his cast iron pan, and it began to melt.

"Coconut oil?" Gayle guessed.

Kellan raised an eyebrow. "Did you see any coconut trees out front? No, it's lard."

Gayle's nose wrinkled again, though she tried to keep a straight face.

"Don't tell me you fell for that farce about lard being bad for your health," he said.

"Um…"

"Lard is only unhealthy if it comes from unhealthy pigs. I render this myself, get the fat from a farmer down the road. His pigs actually get to see the light of day. There's no better fat to get you through wintertime. Best source of vitamin D on the planet. Way better than the super processed, rancid vegetable oil most people use."

Gayle pursed her lips. The Milky Thistle had gone through countless gallons of vegetable oil in order to satisfy demand for French fries and other popular items. It's not as if they could fill the fryer with locally sourced lard.

Kellan moved with ease in his kitchen, happily oblivious to Gayle's sour looks. He seared the fish quickly in the cast iron pan, then plated it and topped it with salt and a squeeze of lemon.

"I didn't see a lemon tree out front," Gayle teased.

Kellan grinned. "Guilty as charged. Citrus is my Achilles

heel. Puts me in mind of pioneers who would buy oranges as Christmas gifts, they were so precious."

"So you do occasionally go to the grocery store," Gayle said as they sat down on stools at the kitchen counter.

"I'm not a purist," Kellan said easily. "I don't deny myself the things that I love. Meyer lemons, coffee, the occasional glass of wine. But usually, the things that I harvest myself or buy from friends are a hell of a lot better than anything you can find at the grocery store."

Gayle took a bite of the fresh fish and found that she had to agree. It was absolutely delicious.

"We have to put this on our menu," she said immediately.

"That good, huh?" Kellan was so close that Gayle could see the gold flecks in his green eyes and feel the heat that radiated from his arm to hers. Her cheeks colored as she turned her eyes back to her plate and took another bite. "I only catch enough to feed myself—and the rare guest—but I might have some friends who could keep you stocked. Any excuse to spend more days fishing."

Just yesterday, Gayle would have dismissed that urge as laziness.

Today, she understood.

They finished their meal in comfortable silence, savoring the flaky fish. Afterward, Kellan opened a bottle of sweet red wine. They put on their coats and went outside, where they sat shoulder to shoulder on the porch swing and watched the stars appear, one at a time, over the forest. Gayle was acutely aware of every small movement that Kellan made, each breath, and the warmth of his thigh against hers as he shifted closer.

Later, when Gayle checked her phone, she was shocked to see how late it was, how quickly this unrushed time with Kellan had passed. Reluctantly, she stood. Without Kellan's warmth and his bulk sheltering her from the wind, the night suddenly felt quite cold.

"I should go. I have an early day tomorrow."

Kellan nodded and stood in turn. He took Gayle's empty wine glass and set it on the table beside his own.

"I like spending time with you," he said simply. His hand was warm and surprisingly gentle as he tucked a stray strand of hair behind Gayle's ear. He leaned towards her and then paused. "Can I kiss you?"

She was shocked to realize that she wanted him to. She gave the barest nod, and he leaned in the rest of the way. The kiss was what she might have expected from Kellan, slow and sure. Undemanding. With the slightest urging, Gayle might have spent the rest of that night in his arms. But instead of pulling her closer, he stepped away.

"Thank you for coming today. Maybe on our next date, I'll show you what I can do with a piece of venison."

Gayle's face blazed with a blush that she hoped was invisible in the moonlight. *Our next date.*

"I'd like that," she said with an affected calm. "See you at work?"

Kellan nodded. "See you there."

Gayle turned and walked away, heart racing. This had been her first date in decades—quite possibly the best date of her life—and she hadn't even realized it was a *date* until it was over.

17

NIKKI

"Knit three, purl two," Nikki muttered over and over again as she went around and around the rim of her first hat. "Knit three... two... one... purl two... one... knit three... purl two..."

She had always been impressed by her daughter's creations, but attempting to knit herself took her admiration of Beth's talents to a whole new level. *How* did she manage to follow those complicated patterns for colorwork hats and cabled sweaters? Beth had left most of her needles and some leftover yarn behind when she left for school. Each project required needles of a different size, and Beth had taken only what she needed for her current works in progress.

With help from some YouTube videos, Nikki had taught herself how to cast on and knit in the round. It had been intensely frustrating at points, but when she got into the groove of the repetitive motion, it could also be soothing, even meditative. She was nowhere near Beth's level of skill, but she had managed to knit a striped baby blanket for her very pregnant neighbor using chunky yarn she'd purchased for that purpose, and she was making decent progress on her first hat using some of Beth's leftover yarn. Knitting, combined with audiobooks, was an excellent distraction for her frazzled mind.

Mateo hadn't dumped her, but the rest of her stay in Bluebird Bay had felt tense.

"I just want to make sure we're on the same page," he'd said. "I don't mean to rush you, and you don't have to be the one to move... but eventually, I want us to be closer together."

Nikki was hesitant to make a commitment to him, to merge her whole life with a man after the prolonged nightmare that she had brought upon herself with Beth's father. Steve had seemed wonderful and charming at first, too, at least to the naive teenager that Nikki had been when they'd met. Then, she'd thrown the rest of her life away and gone all in for him, and Steve had slowly morphed into an absolute monster.

Mateo wasn't Steve, she knew that. Steve had been a psychopath, a narcissistic abuser who had hated his own daughter for drawing Nikki's energy and attention away from him. Mateo was kind and generous, a wonderful father to his grown daughter. And yet... what didn't she know about him? What would change if they lived together, saw each other every day?

Nikki had never been in a healthy relationship. She had been so young when Steve had charmed her away from her family in Cherry Blossom Point, and extricating herself from that nightmare had taken years. Finally, when Steve was locked away and Nikki was safe to return home, she had begun to date a bit... but nothing lasting, nothing serious.

She'd had endless excuses. She needed to focus on her career, and any free time that she had, needed to go to Beth. She would much rather spend time with her wonderful daughter than with some guy. There were no single men worth dating in Cherry Blossom Point anyway. She was a strong independent woman who didn't need no man.

Then, Beth left for college, and Nikki met a wonderful man who wanted to be a true partner to her... and all of those excuses collapsed in on themselves. Nikki was left standing in the wreckage of the walls she'd put up, wondering why she *still* wasn't ready to commit to this man. She had new excuses, but they felt flimsy. It's too soon. Neither of us should uproot our lives.

She loved Mateo. She didn't want to lose him. And bless his heart, the man was patient. But for how long? How long would he put up with Nikki's dithering before he broke things off with her in favor of dating someone right there in Bluebird Bay?

A knock on the door saved Nikki from herself. So much for the distraction of knitting and audiobooks. She had no idea what the narrator had said for at least a chapter or two. Nikki paused it with a sigh and carefully set down her work in progress, sliding the loops of thread off of the needles and onto the length of wire that connected them so that the whole thing wouldn't unravel while her back was turned.

Gayle was standing on her front step. She looked Nikki up and down as she opened the door, pursing her lips at the sight of her baby sister in moose-head pajama pants and fuzzy slippers at two in the afternoon.

"Good, you're home," Gayle said sardonically. She'd been sleeping in Beth's room, but had thrown herself into this new project with Jo so whole-heartedly that they'd hardly seen each other since Nikki got back from Bluebird Bay. Gayle was gone by the time Nikki got up in the mornings and back long after Nikki had gone to bed.

Okay, so maybe Nikki had been spending a *little* too much time in bed.

"Hello to you, too," Nikki said blearily, squinting into the afternoon sunlight that slanted through her front door. "Why did you knock?"

"To see if you were home. And get you off your butt. Get dressed, we're going for a drive."

"Seriously?"

"You have something better to do? A job interview?"

Nikki crossed her arms in front of her chest. She'd been looking for jobs, but had yet to find a single one worth applying to that was less than an hour away.

"That's what I thought," Gayle said. "I'm short on time. Hop to it."

Nikki did as she was told, muttering all the while about ice queens and the axis of evil. Once she was dressed and buckled into Gayle's car, her sister gave her a look of annoyance.

"You lost your job and you didn't even tell me?" Gayle put her car in reverse and pulled out of Nikki's driveway. "I'm staying with you and still I had to hear through Lena that those rat bastards at the Locavore *fired* you?"

"Technically, I quit," Nikki said, looking out at the drab landscape that was March in Maine. Bare trees and dead grass, muddy snow and the withered corpses of a few foolish plants that had shot up between frosts. "They offered to keep me on as a line cook."

"After you created a menu from scratch and trained their entire back of house staff? That is such bullshit!"

"Yep." Grim as she felt, Nikki couldn't help but smile at Gayle's protective anger.

"Why didn't you tell me?"

"I haven't seen you."

"Bullshit. I'm living in your *house*, Nikki. You ran off to Bluebird Bay and then came back and holed up in your room. Why?"

Nikki looked out the window. "Maybe I wasn't ready to hear you say 'I told you so'."

"What?" Gayle shot her a look of profound hurt and looked back to the road. "Why would I say that? I never told you not to take the job. You have no way of knowing they would do this."

Nikki shrugged. Gayle was right; she'd given Nikki no reason to think that she'd tell her those four little words over this latest venture. It was just that Nikki had heard them from her big sister so many thousands of times in her life, her knee jerk response was to shut her out until she'd figured things out for herself.

"Where are we going?" Nikki asked.

"Hunter's Gathering," Gayle said cheerfully.

"Your new bar?"

"Yes, Nikki," Gayle drawled with exaggerated patience, "my new bar."

The place was in the forest just outside of town, not so far that people wouldn't be willing to make the drive. Actually, it was a little bit closer to Nikki's house than the riverside property of her most recent job. Gayle had to maneuver around heavy machinery to park in front of the building; a small bulldozer was pushing brush out of the way, grading the earthen parking lot.

"Man." Nikki stared at the trucks parked here and there and the workers coming in and out of the large building. "You guys are all in on this, huh?"

"In for a penny, in for a pound," Gayle said cheerfully. "Come in and see."

The front room was chaos. Workers, power tools, piled materials. Gayle led Nikki upstairs to a huge room that contained nothing but a neatly organized desk overlooking the building's phenomenal view.

"This will be our dining space," Gayle told her. "The bar and all the fun stuff will be downstairs."

"It's gorgeous."

"Come take a look at the kitchen." She led Nikki downstairs, to the three rooms that they'd knocked dividing walls out of to turn them into one commercial kitchen. "The guy that you recommended was great. He pointed our contractor in the right direction, and together they've made short work of it. But I need you to help with all the details."

"Sure, I can do that," Nikki said listlessly. It wasn't as if she had anything better to do. But still, this would be a *job*. The kitchen was half-finished, some of the new appliances still covered in plastic. She didn't suppose Gayle expected her to work for free, but she also didn't know how much Gayle and Jo could afford, with everything else they had going. "At least, until I find a new job."

"You're not getting it, Nikki. I want you to run our kitchen. Design the menu, everything."

Nikki stared at her sister. "Me?"

"Who else? You're the best there is. I would have offered

you the job from the get go if you hadn't already been running a kitchen. What your old bosses did was shitty, but maybe it's kismet. Now you can partner with Jo and me!"

Nikki stared around the half-finished room, reeling inwardly. Gayle had asked her to run the kitchen at The Milky Thistle years ago, but Nikki had turned her down. She'd told Gayle that running a kitchen of her own wouldn't leave her with enough time for Beth, who was only ten at the time. But the full truth of her refusal had been that working for Gayle had sounded like a nightmare. Gayle had been controlling and overbearing; being her baby sister *and* her employee would have driven Nikki insane.

But now? Gayle had mellowed considerably, and it felt like the two of them were on more equal footing. Sure, Gayle fell into old habits sometimes… but overall, their relationship was in a good place. Nikki was surprised to realize that she *liked* the idea of working with Gayle and Jo. And of course, she wanted a second shot at running her own kitchen. But she and Gayle had *just* redefined their relationship; it was really still a work in progress. What if working for her made things worse instead of better? But really, was she so afraid of that that she'd rather go back to slinging hash in some diner off the interstate?

"I'll think about it," she said cautiously. "Thank you for the offer."

"Thank you for the offer," Gayle mimicked in a formal, robotic voice. She put an arm around Nikki, led her outside to the relatively quiet back side of the building, and settled her onto a bench. They were quiet for a moment. Gayle still had an arm around Nikki, and she leaned her head to one side so that her sleek dark hair rested on Nikki's curls.

"I know you're used to thinking of me as an ice queen," Gayle said gently. "One half of the axis of evil. But I'm trying, kid. I've been doing better, haven't I?"

"Absolutely," Nikki replied. "I'm just afraid that mixing work and family might jinx this new friendship we've got going."

"That's fair." Gayle straightened up with a sigh. "I just want to say that if you sign on, the kitchen is yours. Jo's got some ideas about the theme, and we've already found some sources for local game and the like, but the food and the menu is all you. We trust you."

"Thank you." Nikki knew in her heart that she couldn't turn this down... still, she wanted to sit with the idea for a few days before going all in.

"I'm fine with waiting. You let me know when you decide."

"Thanks, Gayle. Tell me more about Jo's ideas."

Gayle grinned. "Hunter and Gatherer, right? So we want to use as much local stuff as we can, with an emphasis on wild game and foraged foods, like mushrooms. Paleo options, if that's still on trend. Keto? I don't know, that's all you. High quality, but we don't care if it's fancy or not. Jo's envisioning some pretty rustic fare, but I think it would be nice to have some fine dining options for upstairs. Just a simple menu. It would need to change pretty often, based on what we can get each week. But there could be some staples, too—maybe burgers and chowder, like at our old place, but using game meats. Jo's hoping we can get really crazy and use the big stone fireplace for roasting meat, cook outside in the summertime, that sort of thing. But like I said—if you take the job, it's really up to you. Just take the theme and the local meat and run with it. Moose burgers, venison steak, whatever."

Nikki's head was already spinning with ideas for the menu, but she pushed them to the back of her mind to simmer. She'd get them all down on paper, maybe even test some things out before she went back to Gayle with a Yes or a No.

"Would you give me the contact info for the people you're sourcing from? I would need to talk to them about what's available each season, maybe get some meat to experiment with. Wild game is a horse of a different color; it really needs its own recipes."

"No horse meat," Gayle said with mock sternness.

Nikki rolled her eyes. "Ha ha."

Gayle grinned. "Yes, I'll forward you their contact info. Though, our main guy can be difficult to get a hold of."

"And that's not sending off alarm bells for a potential supplier?"

"He's reliable," Gayle said with a wry smile. "He just doesn't keep his phone on him all the time. Doesn't even have a smartphone."

"Old school, huh?"

"In more ways than one." There was an unusual note to Gayle's voice, almost dreamy.

Nikki raised an eyebrow. "Yeah?"

"He took me fly fishing. Oh! And he made this amazing dish with lard and lemons...Could you do something like that, do you think? Charred trout or something that will remind people of camping?"

"Wait just a minute." Nikki laughed. "I see you trying to

drop a bomb and then steer the conversation back to food. I'm not falling for that. You went on a *date*?"

Gayle actually *blushed*. "I guess I did. I didn't necessarily realize that at the time? But... yes. And you know what? I'd like to do it again."

"Yes!" Nikki leaned towards her sister, bumping their shoulders together. "Go, Gayle! Who is this guy?"

"His name is Kellan Hayes." Gayle's voice was quiet and calm, but Nikki could sense an excitement beneath her words. "He's so straightforward. Unnervingly so, sometimes. It's refreshing to meet someone so relentlessly honest. But he's laid back, too. At first, I was worried that he was *too* laid back—probably because Rex was just plain lazy—but you should see what he's built inside! Jo brought him in to build an axe throwing area—"

"Back up," Nikki interrupted. "Axe throwing? Who *are* you?"

Gayle chuckled. "We have some catching up to do. I'm actually pretty good at it. You should try it before we leave today; it's all finished. That's what I was trying to say about Kellan. When he says he'll be there, he's there. And when he starts a project, he finishes it. He wouldn't commit to a timeline when he agreed to build the axe throwing area for us—I was worried it would take him forever—but he's done already. Meanwhile, all the other workers are still smack in the middle of other projects. He's calm and relaxed, but he's not lazy."

"You *liiike* him," Nikki teased, giving Gayle another playful nudge.

Gayle just smiled. "Yeah," she admitted, looking out over the trees. "I do."

18

JACK

Jack's last class on Monday wrapped up at four. Now that he had Corinne waiting for him at home every night, he'd handed the two evening classes off to another teacher. He was transitioning towards focusing more on the survival school and on self-defense teacher training courses; his employees could handle the basic self-defense courses. Last year, working seventy hours a week had been necessary to fill his life with purpose and meaning. This year, he was happy to work forty—okay, fifty, but he was moving in the right direction—hours each week and spend that extra time with Corinne... or with his therapist.

Never in a million years would Jack have imagined himself in therapy. As a nebulous concept, the idea still grated on him. It's a good thing he liked the grief counselor Corinne had set him up with. And despite the niggling shame that he still carried at being the sort of person who *needed* therapy, he was deeply grateful for how his life had transformed in such a short time. If he could only get things sorted with Wyatt...

Jack took a detour on his way home; Gayle had been hounding him to stop by her new place and check out the progress she'd made thus far. And Jack hadn't even set eyes on the place. He owed her a visit, even just a quick one. Jack liked the building the minute he saw it. It hardly looked like a restaurant, but people went in for that sort of thing these days. Not just another diner. The anti-strip mall.

"Jackdaw!" Gayle crowed as he opened the door to his truck. It was his childhood nickname, dusty with disuse, but it got a smile from Jack. Eric had called him that from the time he was small, had given each of his children their own avian name—maybe it was as close as he could get to giving them the wings he'd so sorely wanted. The jackdaw was a black bird—basically, a crow. The old nickname gave Jack a sudden flashback to Eric's quiet urging, well over twenty years ago now, to work things out with Corinne.

"Jackdaws mate for life, son."

The old man was wise, even back then.

"Hey, sister," Jack greeted her.

"You finally came. I wasn't sure you would."

Jack bristled slightly at that. He had flaws a-plenty, but being unreliable was not one of them. "I said I would."

"Come on inside. It's a mess, but we've accomplished so much already."

It was good to see Gayle looking so vibrant. She looked younger than she had in years. The divorce had knocked her down, but she'd jumped right back to her feet and seemed to be doing better than ever. She'd thrown herself into this project, steadfast friend by her side, and it was doing her a world of good.

"Those stairs go up to the dining room," Gayle said as she led him inside. "It's a bit more bougie up there. Think date nights, big family dinners, weekend brunches. But over *here*," she continued, leading him off to the left, "is the bar."

It was a huge space. A long wooden bar, half finished, stretched the length of the northern wall. To the east, large windows looked out onto the forest. Booths were being built along the front wall, and there was plenty of space in the middle for more tables. At the far end, there were several rows of fencing supported by thin wooden columns. Gayle led Jack across the room, talking on and on about her plans for tables and chairs and games and drinks. Kellan Hayes was there, putting the finishing touches on the axe throwing area he'd built. He grinned when he saw them.

"Hey there, Gayle. Jack. Ready to test out the axe lanes?"

Jack grinned. "It's been a while."

"We've just got the one axe," Kellan said, handing it over. Jack hefted it, feeling its weight and balance. It was well made, and sharp.

"That's an interesting business strategy," he said, for no reason other than to annoy his sister. "Are you going to auction it off at the beginning of the night, or...?"

"Ha ha," Gayle said. She took the axe from his hand, lined herself up, and tossed it. It hit the target—and not too far from the center, either. Jack raised his eyebrows.

"How is it that you can't throw a dart to save your life, but suddenly you're a Viking warrior with the axe?"

Kellan laughed at that, and Gayle's eyes narrowed.

"Sorry," Kellan said, still chuckling. "I'm not laughing at

you. I'm picturing what a real Viking would have to say about these puny little axes. It's like something they would've given a five year old as a toy."

Gayle's eyes narrowed further, but her mouth twitched in amusement. "Good thing you're not in charge of publicity."

Jack walked down the lane and retrieved the axe, then walked back and tried for himself. The thing rotated a bit too far, and hit the target —in the middle, for the record— with its flat side. It rebounded and fell to the ground with a clatter.

"You were standing too far away," Gayle told him. She looked to Kellan. "Do you think we should paint lines on the floor?"

"Nah, let them figure it out. You'll probably have axes of different weights and lengths in the long run, anyway, and they'll have to stand at different distances. Don't want to make it too easy for them or they'll stop coming back."

Gayle smiled at him. "Fair enough."

There was an energy between the two that gave Jack pause.

Could it be...? Mountain-man Kellan and his prissy sister? No way in hell. He walked down to retrieve the axe once again.

"Did you want to give us a demonstration, Kellan?"

"I think Gayle's demonstration was adequate," he replied.

"I'll give it a go." Jo walked up, wearing her usual faded jeans and a plaid shirt. Now, Jo and Kellan, that would make sense. But that indescribable energy that Jack had noticed between Kellan and Gayle was nowhere to be seen as the man made way for Jo—going to stand, Jack noticed, right next to his sister. He handed Jo the axe and stepped aside. She threw it casually, one handed, and it hit the target dead center. Gayle whooped and applauded.

"It's no wonder you were so set on this," she said playfully. "It's just another way for you to fleece unsuspecting tourists."

"Is that so?" said Kellan.

Gayle grinned at him. "You should have seen her playing darts at The Milky Thistle. Tourists in the summer, young townies in the wintertime. I never saw her lose a game."

The way she was smiling up at Kellan made the hair stand up on the back of Jack's neck. But it was a ridiculous instinct. This was a fifty-year-old woman, not some little girl—not that he could ever look at Gayle and *not* see the ten-year-old who was always stealing his hockey skates. She knew how to take care of herself, and she deserved to be happy. And if anyone he knew deserved her, it was Kellan Hayes.

"Oh, I lost once or twice," Jo said.

"How are you with a bow?" Jack asked her. "You want a job this summer?"

Jo smirked. "You couldn't afford me," she said, and everyone laughed. She and Kellan got back to work, and Gayle showed Jack the kitchen and the upstairs dining area. It was relatively quiet upstairs, and they sat at one of the tables that overlooked the forest. It was a wet, drizzly day, the kind some might regard as dreary... but Jack had always thought that silver skies over the dark green forest was one of the most beautiful sights in the world. They were quiet for a moment, enjoying the view. Jack thought of the phenomenal space that Gayle had created at The Milky Thistle and wondered if that loss dampened the excitement of creating a new place... if a part of her was holding back on this second endeavor after the loss of the first.

He said, "It's weird for me, driving past The Milky Thistle and knowing I'll never step foot in there again. It must be a hundred times harder for you."

"It sucks," Gayle admitted easily. "This place saved me. I was going crazy, trying to fill my time. I wouldn't have been ready to start from scratch on my own. Maybe ever. But Jo roped me into this place before I sunk too low, and it's been a godsend. I'm so excited about it. It doesn't make what happened with our old place hurt any less, but it leaves me without any time to dwell on it, you know? Having something else to pour my energy into makes all the difference."

Jack nodded. He understood that feeling.

"How about you? Have you heard from Wyatt?"

"I called him and he actually picked up."

"That's great! How is he?"

"Good, I think. He says school is going well, and he seems really happy there."

"So why do you seem so down?"

"It took about two minutes for me to completely botch the conversation."

Gayle grimaced sympathetically. "How's that?"

"I said something about those insanely dangerous jumps that he does to impress strangers online."

"Jack," Gayle groaned, turning his name into a reprimand.

"Well, I didn't say it like *that*. I just said something about safety precautions—"

"But that was what he heard. Yeah, I get it. Our kids hear the meaning... the *intention* and feeling beneath our words.

Sometimes they're more aware of it than we are. It was the same with me and Maddy when she was that age. Even now, I can't make the slightest suggestion without her taking it as this dire insult and shutting me out. It's my own fault, I guess. I was too critical of her growing up." She laughed, but it was a sad sound. "I thought I was helping."

"I just want him to be safe," Jack said, looking out at the trees. He had been so terrified of losing his second son that he had pushed him away. Had he ruined his last chance with Wyatt?

"It's not too late," Gayle said, answering his unspoken question. "He'll be home soon for Easter break, yeah?"

Jack nodded. "In a few days, yeah. He said he'd meet up for a meal, but that was before I botched things." Words didn't come easy to Jack, but he'd had some practice with communicating his emotions this past winter. "I don't know if he'll still want to see me. And even if he does, I'm scared that I'll say something to mess things up again, like I did on our call."

When he looked over at Gayle, she was staring at him with a strange expression on her face. There was loving sympathy there, but a glint of amusement, too.

He frowned at her. "What?"

"Look at us, talking about real stuff and real emotions like grownups. We're *sharing*."

Jack grimaced. "If you're going to call it that, I'll never do it again."

Gayle grinned at him. "It's good, Jack. Old dogs, new tricks. I'm proud of us."

"I am not an old dog," he growled. Gayle just laughed. She wasn't old, either. In fact, she looked more alive and beautiful than she had all through her long marriage with Rex.

"You look good, Gayle. Happy. It's good to see you happy."

She smiled at him. "It's good to see you happy, too. It warms my heart whenever I see you and Corinne together. I'm really proud of you for all the work you've done to heal."

"On that note," Jack said, standing, "I should get going. Corinne's making fettuccine alfredo."

"Yum."

"Do you want to come? She always makes way more than we need. Probably because she's used to cooking for a teenager. I don't mind the leftovers, but, well. There's room at the table."

"No," Gayle said easily, "you enjoy your dinner with Corinne. I have a mountain of paperwork to deal with before I head back to Nikki's, and you know that house is always full of food. But why don't you and Corinne come to Nikki's house tomorrow? She's been cooking up a storm, experimenting with venison and trout and stuff. You know how she gets after life deals her a blow, just cooks her way through it. I brought all the construction workers lunch today just to make some room in the fridge." She wrinkled her nose, just as she had as a little kid. "The moose lasagna was edible, but definitely not good enough to make it onto the menu."

"I'd like that, but tomorrow doesn't work for me. I'm picking Dad up after his flight lesson with Anna, and I figured I'd take them out to dinner."

Gayle's eyes went wide. "*Them?* Are you for real right now?"

"I just thought... I could ask, at least." Jack shrugged and looked away. He wasn't proud of how he'd treated their half-sister... there were amends to be made there, too.

"Will wonders never cease," Gayle murmured.

Jack turned to go, then looked back at her. "By the way... I noticed that while we were *sharing*," he put the word in finger quotes, "you failed to mention that you have a major crush on Kellan Hayes."

Her jaw actually dropped. She caught herself a fraction of a second later and shut her mouth, blinking at him in shock.

"And," he pressed, "even though you didn't ask, I want you to know that I approve. He's a good man. The only one I can think of who might be good enough for you."

As he walked away, Gayle squawked behind him, "What are you talking about? It's not like that. Well, not really. And I don't need your *approval*, Jack. You're the younger twin, in case you forgot. I'm a good ten minutes older and wiser than you!"

Jack grinned and trotted down the stairs without a backwards glance. He'd only mentioned it to test his theory, and Gayle had confirmed it for him. Without a doubt. Busted.

19

GAYLE

Gayle's cheeks blazed pink as she stomped across the room to her workspace. The nerve of that man... thought he knew everything about her just because he'd known her for fifty years... Stupid Jack. Gayle sank into her chair with a sigh. Was she *that obvious?* If so, she needed to rein it in some. She heaved another dramatic sigh, taking advantage of having the spacious second floor all to herself. Then, she shoved aside thoughts of men and dove into her paperwork. Invoices, payroll, projections... it was nothing she hadn't handled before, but starting from scratch felt overwhelming. Still, she was more than competent. It wasn't long before she found her groove. Getting through all of this would take hours, but she didn't much mind. It would keep her busy, keep her thoughts from straying elsewhere. Time passed quickly when she was occupied.

"Gayle?"

She looked up in surprise. She hadn't heard Kellan come up the stairs.

"You're the last one working again," he told her with a gentle smile. "Everyone else has gone home. I had a bit left to do, but I'm done."

"For the day?" Gayle asked.

"Done with the project," he clarified.

"Oh. Great," Gayle said flatly.

Kellan gave her another slow, knowing smile. "Come out to dinner with me."

"Tonight?" Gayle looked down at all of the numbers yet to be sorted. She looked back up and Kellan was waiting patiently, watching her with that smile that she couldn't quite figure out. Gayle thought suddenly of that night on his front porch, that sure and steady kiss.

"I could eat." Gayle closed her laptop and set it on top of the paperwork. "Where did you have in mind?"

"There's a new place I've been wanting to try. My neighbor sells them pork. Apparently, it's all local food."

"Le Four Locavore?" Gayle asked.

"That's the one. I've heard great things."

"I bet," Gayle huffed. "My sister was their head chef all winter. They had her take on the brunt of the work, write up the seasonal menus, train the staff—and then they dumped her for their cousin."

Kellan raised his eyebrows in surprise, but a second later, that subtle smile returned to his face. He was looking at Gayle with a sort of appreciation that made her heart rate rise.

"You're beautiful when you're angry."

Gayle just frowned at him. He'd said something like that before.

"So the Locavore's out," Kellan said. "How about La Traviata?"

"Sure." Gayle felt a sudden rush of affection for this man and his immense patience. With Rex, a single scowl from Gayle would have been enough for him to give her the cold shoulder for the rest of the week. Kellan just stood there, patient and smiling, and told her she was beautiful.

Was this guy for real?

She grinned and grabbed her purse up off the floor.

"Just for the record," Kellan said as they walked down the stairs, "you're beautiful when you smile, too."

La Traviata was a phenomenal Italian restaurant on Main Street. They drove past The Milky Thistle to get there, but Gayle didn't so much as glance at it. Though she couldn't help but notice that there were far more free parking spaces available than there had ever been when *she* was running the place.

When they got to La Traviata, the restaurant was only half full, and they were able to get a table right away. Gayle knew how crowded the place got towards the end of the week, and she was grateful for the relative quiet. Low opera music played in the background as the waiter brought two glasses of water and fresh bread.

The menu was short, but everything on it looked phenomenal. Homemade pasta and slow braised meats. She felt a twinge of grief as she looked over the *affettati misti*—her own cured meat platters had been the talk of the town, once—but no matter. She'd be serving up her own food soon enough.

"Shall we start with the *finocchio all'arancia*?" Kellan

asked. Gayle found it on the menu, thinly shaved fennel with orange slices.

"Yum. Yes." She read through the menu for another minute. "I can't decide between the lobster ravioli or the gnocchi or the osso buco... They all look so good."

"Get all three," Kellan said with a grin.

Gayle laughed. "What?"

"We'll share." He set his menu down and waved to the waiter. After they ordered their food and wine and the server walked away, Gayle grinned at him across the table.

"I can't believe we ordered three entrees."

Kellan shrugged, still smiling. "I go out to dinner about twice a year. Might as well go all out. Anyway," he said quietly, "have you seen what passes for dinner portions at places like this? A working man needs two entrees just to fill his belly."

He tore a roll in two and spread a liberal amount of butter on each half, then offered one to Gayle. She took it with a smile, blushing as her fingers brushed Kellan's.

They didn't speak much as they ate. Kellan seemed content to enjoy the music and Gayle's company; he watched her with a steadiness that made Gayle uneasy... but in a way that made her want to get closer to him, not in a way that made her want to bolt.

The ravioli and the slow-braised pork osso buco were both delicious, but the *gnocchi al quattro formaggi* left them both in the dust. The luscious cream sauce was almost too decadent, but it was nicely balanced by Gayle's red wine and the occasional bite of fennel. After their decadent dinner, they still managed to polish off a generous slice of tiramisu.

"That's the best dinner I've had in ages," Gayle said,

swiping the last dab of coffee-flavored cream off the plate that sat between her and Kellan, "and I live with a chef!"

Across the table, Kellan froze. "Oh?"

Gayle chuckled, delighted to see him discomfited, for once. "I'm staying with my little sister. I've been so busy with work that I still haven't found a new place to live. Sold the family house a couple months ago."

Kellan smiled at her. He started to say something, but just then, the owner and head chef of La Traviata walked up to their table and set down a second dessert.

"Limoncello cake, on the house."

"Stan," Gayle protested with a laugh, "we just ate three entrees and the tiramisu."

"I could keep going," Kellan said, diving into the pale yellow cake.

"Good man," Stan said. He turned to Gayle. "I just wanted to say how sorry I was to hear about The Milky Thistle. I heard it isn't going so well there. Jimmy and his kitchen staff walked out when the place changed hands—I hear he's opening up his own burger joint this summer—and the quality of the food went downhill fast. They broke it off with all your local distributors and went for the cheap stuff. It's a mess. They still get some bar traffic since they're open later than anyone else in town, but that's it. It's a ghost town at dinnertime."

Gayle nodded, working to hide an elated grin that threatened to erupt.

"I've gotta get back, but it was good to see you. Keep us posted on that new place that you and Jo are working on, will you? Tina and I will be there for the grand opening."

"Thanks, Stan. We're planning a soft opening, too, for

friends and family. As soon as the kitchen's up and running. I'll send you an invitation as soon as we can pin down a date."

"Sounds good!"

Stan walked away and Gayle looked at Kellan, who was watching her with one of those slow-burning smiles spreading across his face.

"What?" she demanded.

"I don't know about you," he drawled, "but if my ex all but stole my bar out from under me and was running it into the ground inside two months, I'd be celebrating. Champagne?"

Gayle laughed and nodded. She liked that, even though Kellan seemed almost preternaturally calm and even tempered, he had a little bit of a wicked side, too. He flagged down their server.

"We're ready for the check—but first, would it be possible to get a bottle of champagne to go?"

"Yes sir, I'll be right back." The young man walked away and Gayle regarded Kellan with one raised eyebrow.

"Where are we going?"

Kellan's smile was enigmatic. "You'll see."

They climbed into his truck and he drove out of town and a little ways up the side of the mountain. He drove down a dirt road and parked at the edge of a meadow. Without a word, he climbed out of the car and circled around to open the door for Gayle. She buttoned her coat over her sweater as Kellan grabbed a blanket out of the truck and headed into the meadow, champagne in hand. He spread out the blanket and popped the champagne a few feet away, so that the sudden spray of bubbles landed on the earth. Kellan took a long swig and held the bottle to Gayle, who took a cautious sip.

A FRESH START

"If this is meant to be a seduction, Kellan Hayes—" she began, intending to tell him that they were too old, it was too cold, he had a perfectly adequate house, for goodness sake—but he held out one finger and put it over her mouth, so softly that she barely felt it at all.

"Look up," he said.

Gayle gave him a reactionary scowl—Kellan just grinned broader—and then looked up at the sky.

It was exquisite. The moon was a thin crescent, and she could see the milky way. A shooting star streaked by at the corner of her vision, and then another. A meteor shower. This was what he'd brought her out here to see.

Kellan sat down on the blanket and patted the space next to him. They lay back, watching the enduring magic of shooting stars. It was amazing, like nothing Gayle had seen in decades. She'd never taken the time. Kellan pulled her closer, inviting her to use the comfortable space below his shoulder as a pillow.

And to think, *she* had tried to tell Kellan Hayes about seduction.

20

LENA

Lena sat in bed with her computer, wrestling with yet another graphic design app. She was trying to feature a variety of projects in a banner ad, but it always wound up looking clunky and amateurish. She was beginning to think that the problem wasn't with the endless succession of free and premium sites she had tried, but rather with her abilities as a graphic designer... or lack thereof.

Owen thundered up the stairs and into the apartment, where Lena took one look at his sweat-soaked work shirt and pointed to the shower.

"We have ten minutes before we need to leave for the gallery," she told him, snapping her laptop shut. She stood up from the bed and met Owen in the middle of the room to give him a kiss that belied her scolding. "It's forty-two minutes away."

He gave her a slow grin and pulled at the belt of her robe. "Will you be joining me, then?"

Lena laughed and shoved him towards the bathroom. "I

just took a shower. We're not going to be late for the opening. Go on."

Owen grunted in good-natured disappointment and gave Lena a firm kiss on the lips before retreating to the bathroom. Lena pulled on her favorite pair of pants—dark gray, stretchy, swanky jeans that had been worth every exorbitant penny. In the past, she had gravitated towards high-fashion clothes that hid her figure beneath swaths of lightweight fabric. These days, accompanied everywhere she went by a man who loved her every curve, she had drifted towards the simpler pieces in her wardrobe, the ones that hugged her curves instead of hiding them. She looked in the closet for a moment—only a small portion of her wardrobe actually fit in the closet here at the studio—and chose a sweater that she saved for special occasions. A sky blue cashmere, thin and heaven-soft, but still warm enough for a spring evening in Maine. She had been to this gallery a dozen times before and knew it to be a high-ceilinged, poorly heated sort of place. Which was still better than the stifling heat of the tiny Cherry Blossom Point gallery on a crowded opening night.

Clad only in a towel, Owen came up behind her with an appreciative growl. "You look gorgeous."

Lena let him distract her for a moment, thoroughly enjoying the feel of his hands caressing the cashmere that clung to her skin—and then she pulled away with a coquettish smile.

"Five minutes."

"I can get dressed in two," Owen insisted, pulling her in for a kiss. "I feel like I haven't seen you in days."

It was true. Despite living together, they had both been so busy with work that they hardly saw each other except for a late dinner of takeout—and more often than not, they fell asleep the moment they went to bed. Owen had been busy preparing for tonight's show and then catching up on custom orders, and Lena had been up to her eyeballs in code. Trying to figure out the best ways to drive traffic to her website and simultaneously manage a half-dozen social media accounts was driving her slightly mad. Christmas sales had been gangbusters, and this year's holiday season would be even better, but she had to figure out how to boost sales between now and then. Easter was just around the corner, and orders for baskets weren't nearly as good as she'd hoped. She simply didn't have enough hours in the day to network with new artists, update the site, create her own ads, manage the books... just thinking of her to-do list gave her a headache. She returned a lingering kiss from Owen and slipped away.

"I miss you, too," she said, backing towards the bathroom. "Let's get there on time and leave early, okay? We'll pick up some Thai food on the way home, and I won't open my computer until tomorrow. Deal?"

"Deal." Owen picked up a pair of jeans and dropped his towel, making it *very* difficult for Lena to walk away and finish getting ready herself. But she did. A touch of makeup, some turquoise earrings, done. Her hair was an untamed halo of yellow light around her head... one more thing about her appearance that she had come to love over the past winter. It was amazing what ceaseless, sincere compliments from Owen McKenna could do for a girl's self-image.

"Ready?" she asked, stepping back out into the main room.

"Yes, ma'am." Owen was almost unbearably handsome in blue jeans and a dark gray sweater. The thick wool only accentuated his broad chest and strong muscles. Owen had always been good looking, even as a skinny teenager, and the physical work of glassblowing had only made him even more gorgeous.

"You look amazing." Lena was sorely tempted to throw their plans to the wind... but that wasn't a viable option. Owen's latest art would be on display tonight, a playful under-the-sea collection that Lena felt was his best work yet. He'd been experimenting with painting over the glass. Owen was a phenomenal illustrator, which is what had made him such a successful tattoo artist until he'd gotten tired of that line of work and jumped ship to glass blowing. This collection included plates adorned with nautiluses and cuttlefish, a platter gripped by a life-sized octopus, and vases covered by a never-ending school of tropical fish swimming around and around.

But it wasn't just Owen. The large gallery would have work from a number of different artists. Some of them were already featured on Lena's website, but many weren't. It was the perfect opportunity to network, and Lena slid a thick stack of business cards into the pocket of her jeans.

Owen offered her his arm. "Shall we?"

The drive passed quickly as they caught up on everything they hadn't had the chance to talk about over the course of their work-crazed week. Owen rested his hand on Lena's leg and she put her hand over his, absent-mindedly caressing his skin as they talked. This man's friendship had always been the backbone of Lena's life, but the newer joy of making constant physical contact even through mundane conversations? It still lit up her brain like a Christmas tree.

Gemma and her boys were waiting just inside the front

doors when they arrived there to show their support for Owen. The boys were absolutely *giddy* as they greeted them, talking over each other in their excitement to share news of their new dog.

"We named him Ollie," Aiden said.

"And we're pretty sure we can keep him," Liam added, "because the vet said he wasn't microchipped—"

"And we haven't gotten any calls about our signs or the Facebook post Mom put up or anything—"

"I already taught him *sit* and *down* and *stay*," Liam said earnestly. "He is *so* smart."

Lena couldn't help but take on some of their excitement. Surely, if the dog's previous owner was going to claim him, it would have happened already? It had been over a week, and the perfect joy embodied by the Golden Retriever seemed to have done this family some good already. Lena was grateful that they had a new companion.

"It sounds like you've got yourselves a dog," Owen said cheerfully. He shot a questioning look towards his sister.

Gemma smiled—an actual smile—and said, "He's a good dog."

Owen put an arm around her shoulder. "Have you been here long?"

"No, we just got here a minute before you did."

"Where's your stuff, Uncle Owen?" Aiden asked.

"Come on, I'll show you." Owen led the boys off, and Lena greeted Gemma with a hug. Lena saw a half-dozen artists milling around, people that she was desperate to meet and speak to about representing their work on her site... but she was loath to leave Gemma's side. The younger woman seemed more present than last week, but still utterly exhausted. There were dark circles under her eyes, and she moved like the air was thick as water.

"How's it going?" Lena asked. Gemma reacted with a minute, almost invisible flinch, and Lena immediately wished that she hadn't asked.

"It's going," Gemma replied, looking across the room at what was left of her family. "I'm glad we found Ollie. He gives the boys something to focus on. Aiden wanted to sleep with him, but Ollie keeps jumping up on my bed. He cuddles right up to me, on top of the sheets, keeps inching up until he can rest his head on my belly or curl up against my back. I don't mind it. It's better than sleeping alone. The bed is so big..."

Lena felt heartsick for the woman, not even forty and already a widow. It was good that she had a companion to fill her days, but she needed more.

"Have you considered going back to work?" Lena asked.

"I have," Gemma said quietly, "but I'm not sure where to start. I made a terrible impression at the company in Boston, and my boss back in Denver is still angry at me for quitting on them. I can't count on good recommendations from either of them. There are plenty of jobs I could do remotely, but they're all so soul-sucking. I just don't have the energy. I need a job that will give me a reason to get up in the morning, not one that makes me want to crawl back under the covers the minute the boys climb on their bus."

"Do you want to work with me?"

Gemma looked at her in surprise.

"I've created more work for myself than I can handle. I know it's not what you're used to, you've been handling a whole team... but it would be easy for you, just something to do part-time. I need help with ads, site updates, bookkeeping... I should really start my own newsletter, get a mailing list together. Honestly, the list is endless. For everything I accomplish, I add another five things that need to get done."

Gemma smiled, and in that grin Lena saw a hint of Owen, a flash of the freckle-faced kid sister they used to take to the lake in the summertime. She had been just like her big brother, so full of energy and joy. It pained Lena to see her so low, and she knew how heavily it weighed on Owen. He'd been having recurring nightmares lately of Gemma and the kids in the car crash, dreams in which he had to pull them from the truck before they all burned. The night before, he'd woken up crying from a particularly distressing dream in which his late parents were scolding him for failing to take good care of his family. He'd called Gemma that morning and arranged to take the boys for the whole weekend... then hung up and confided to Lena that taking the boys and leaving Gemma behind only tore his guts up all the worse. But she never wanted to go anywhere, never wanted to leave the house... or her bed. It meant a lot that she had put in the effort to show up tonight.

"What do you think?" Lena asked.

"That sounds like fun," Gemma said, "and it would definitely break up the too-long days. I need *something* to do while the boys are in school."

"Great! I would love your help. Maybe we could sit down together next week and brainstorm?"

"Sounds good," Gemma agreed. A glint of humor flashed in her tired eyes as she added, "*Mi casa es tu casa.* Literally."

21

JACK

Jack arrived at the airfield early and got out to stretch his legs. He was standing off to one side as a small plane landed and Anna jumped out. She went to help Eric, but he managed on his own. The man seemed to have gotten ten years younger since his youngest child had gone and dragged Anna into the family. Meeting his long-lost daughter had lifted a weight from his shoulders that his other children had never even realized that he carried. Seeing what an extraordinarily positive impact Anna had had on their father, Jack felt a new rush of shame at the way he had treated her.

Their family had always been divided into two factions. Jack and Gayle had been close to their mother, and their younger sisters had been daddy's girls. That hairline fracture that split the family had finally cracked after their mother's death, when Eric revealed his long-ago infidelity. Jack and Gayle had been furious with him for betraying their mother, and deeply hurt by a lifetime of lies and secrets... but Eric had been such a great father to them in every other way, they'd had no real outlet for their anger. They couldn't unleash it on the old man. Then, Anna had come to town and shouldered her way into the family, and Jack's reaction had been... harsh. He wouldn't blame Anna if she wanted nothing to do with him. But he had to try to make amends. Anna wasn't to blame for any of it, hadn't even known about their family until *after* Eric revealed his lifelong secret and Nikki went searching for their long-lost sister. The fact was, Anna was family, whether he liked the way she'd been conceived or not. He'd been wrong to try to stonewall her.

Jack walked to greet Eric and Anna as they walked away from the plane.

"How was it?" he asked.

"Exhilarating," Eric replied. "I'm starved."

"I made reservations at your favorite seafood place," Jack replied. He looked at Anna and was struck dumb by her hazel eyes, so exactly like their father's. She looked so much like their younger sister that it still spooked him. Struggling to find his voice, Jack said, "Are you coming?"

"Me?" Anna raised her eyebrows. "Is that your idea of an invitation?"

Jack chuckled and looked away, running a hand over his hair. Leave it to him to sound like an ass even just inviting his long-lost sister to dinner. This wasn't easy, but Jack had to admit it. He liked her spirit.

"I guess it was." He looked back at his half-sister. "The place is called Sea View. Dad loves their chowder, and they have the best fresh oysters around. I made a reservation for three. Would you like to have dinner with us?"

Anna gave him a long, appraising look. Then, she grinned. "Sure."

Jack had never seen his dad look quite so happy. Eric looked more excited for this than he had been when Jack dropped him off for his first flying lesson... though that excitement had been tinged with anxiety. This latest thrill, though? Pure joy. Jack could kick himself for not doing this months ago. But he hadn't been ready then. Well, no time like the present.

"The place is half an hour east of here," he told Anna. "Do you want to follow us in your car?"

"How about *we* follow *you*?" she asked with a devilish grin. "We're halfway through the Hamilton soundtrack and Dad is *into* it."

The look Eric gave him was so wide-eyed and joyful that it was almost boyish. "Did you know that there's a musical about our founding father Alexander Hamilton? It is *excellent*."

Jack laughed. "Fine, follow me, then." He was happy to make the drive in silence, anyway, and he'd have a chance to talk to Eric on the way back to Cherry Blossom Point. They rendezvoused at the Sea View restaurant, and for a while their talk centered around food. Jack ordered a dozen mussels for the table... and then another when he and Anna polished them off in under a minute.

"None of my sisters — of our sisters —" Jack caught himself too late, stumbled, and started over with a sheepish grin. "Gayle and Lena and Nikki won't touch oysters," he said, "unless they're fried."

"Even Nikki?"

"Even the chef," he confirmed.

Eric laughed. "The first time you tried one, you said it was like eating slime."

"I was six," Jack protested.

"I mean, I get that," Anna said. "But it's such delicious slime. Especially with horseradish," she added, adorning her next oyster with fresh horseradish puree and lemon.

"They're better than a multivitamin, that's for sure."

"Absolutely. I feel like superwoman when I eat these things."

"You're an adventurous eater, then?" Jack asked awkwardly. Sitting here with the product of his father's affair felt unnatural, but he was trying. This is what people did when they went out to dinner, right? Asked their companions about themselves?

"You have no idea," Anna said, grinning. "I've been around. I've eaten things you couldn't imagine. I made something of a hobby of it in my twenties, to be honest. I traveled so much and to such remote places, there was always something new to try."

"Let's hear it."

Anna shrugged and swallowed another oyster. "Snake soup, tripe tacos, guinea pig, moose heart, fat-bottomed ants... The absolute weirdest thing I've eaten might be kiviak. Now *that* one took some courage, I'll tell you."

"*What* is kiviak?" Jack asked.

Anna looked at the waiter approaching with their food and laughed. "Remind me to tell you when we're not eating. It actually tasted okay, like sweet cheese."

Jack frowned at her, bewildered, but he respected her request as they tucked into their food. Eric ate his favorite clam and haddock chowder; he didn't have much of an appetite these days and usually took the bulk of his food home as leftovers, but he was eating well tonight. Jack ordered the grilled swordfish with crispy Maine potatoes... which he almost regretted as he watched Anna dig into a steamed lobster. She'd requested extra garlic butter, which she poured liberally over both the shellfish and the vegetables that adorned her plate.

Jack was quiet as Eric peppered Anna with questions that they hadn't had time for during the lesson. He wanted to know everything about every bird she had photographed and about her current life in Bluebird Bay. He asked after people by name as if he knew them. Teddy—*That was... Anna's boyfriend's grandson?*—was doing well, apparently, as was her boyfriend, Beckett. Other names went by that Jack wasn't sure of. Stephanie, Todd, Max... As she and Eric talked, Anna caught Jack looking covetously at her lobster and set a large hunk of butter-drenched meat on his plate without so much as pausing her conversation with Eric.

It was delicious.

Jack tried to think of something interesting to ask for courtesy's sake—he didn't want to be thought unfriendly for sitting there without saying a word. Plenty of people had mistaken his natural stoicism for ill temper, and he didn't want Anna to get the wrong idea, or think that he was freezing her out the first time he actually volunteered to spend time with her...

When their conversation ebbed, Jack asked, "How are flying lessons going?"

Anna beamed. "It's a blast. My friend's a phenomenal teacher."

Eric's eyes were distant. "There just aren't words that can describe it. That moment when your wheels leave the tarmac, the feeling of getting airborne... And the *sky* today, Jackdaw.

So clear. That expanse of endless horizon about the green forest, the blue ocean..." He trailed off and shook his head.

"The view from the front of the plane knocks anything you can see from a little passenger window out of the water," Anna said, and then chuckled. "It's bumpy, though, in those little planes. One hell of a ride."

"It's glorious," Eric said with reverence.

"Landing is terrifying," Anna said, laughing again. "But it's a blast."

"Excuse me a moment," Eric said. "I need the restroom. Order me a blueberry crisp if the waiter comes by, would you? A la mode."

Jack caught Anna's eye as Eric walked away. "It's been years since he had such a healthy appetite."

Anna just grinned. "I need to pee, too. Order me that orange cheesecake. Please."

Jack smiled at her crazy curls—so similar to Nikki's—as she walked away. He perused the dessert menu. He hardly ever bothered with dessert—or he hadn't in a very long while, until Corinne showed up. She and Kiera had baked up a storm while she was in town. Maybe just this once...

The waiter came by and Jack gave him Eric and Anna's orders, plus a sticky toffee pudding with bourbon sauce for himself.

"And three coffees, please."

"Sure thing," he said brightly.

Jack took out his phone to check the time and saw that he'd missed a text message from Sadie.

Wyatt will be home in two days. If you can tell me a good day for you to spend time with him, I'll plan around it.

Jack began texting back a long reply detailing the days

and times he had classes and when he was free... then deleted the whole thing.

Any day, he told her. *I'll make sure I'm available.*

Sadie replied with a thumbs up and a smile, and Jack felt more hopeful than he had in a long time.

22

JACK

Much to Jack's delight, Wyatt answered another video chat from him the day before his flight. Jack cautiously lobbed the notion of survival training, one on one, as something they could do together that might be more interesting than an awkward, stilted conversation for forty minutes at some burger joint. He'd received Wyatt's shocking and enthusiastic agreement with a grin so wide it felt like his face might split. Jack had confirmed the date with Sadie, careful not to step on her plans, and thought of nothing else in the days since. Where should they go? Would the weather stay unseasonably warm, or would they get another cold snap? Which skills should they focus on in the tiny amount of time that they had? Jack sketched up some plans that he eventually crumpled into a ball and binned. Better to let Wyatt choose. He didn't want to cause the kid to shut down immediately by pushing his own agenda.

Jack got to the survival cabin early on the day that he was to meet up with his son. Jack made both coffee and hot chocolate, not knowing which one the boy preferred now, at age seventeen. Hell, the kid lived in Europe... maybe he only drank tea. Jack should have brought tea... Corinne had filled an entire kitchen cabinet with the stuff.

As six o'clock approached, Jack paced nervously within the confines of the cabin. He glanced at his watch every thirty seconds or so. Six o'clock came and went. The sun rose, the birds sang in a raucous chorus all around the cabin... and nothing. Jack checked his phone, a useless habit—it didn't get reception out here.

Five minutes past... no big deal. Maybe they made a wrong turn.

Ten minutes past...

Twelve...

Wyatt changed his mind. What teenager wanted to spend his few days stateside off in the backwoods with his dad, trying to start a fire in the frigid Maine air without a lighter or matches... of course, Jack did *have* both, just in case, but—

Jack was rescued from the idle prattle of his worry by the sound of tires crunching on gravel. He glanced quickly at his watch as he headed for the door. Fourteen minutes past the hour.

Jack opened the door to see his long-limbed son unfolding himself, rising up from Sadie's little car. His breath rose in clouds of steam, white against the dark backdrop of evergreens. Maine was fickle like that. There were years that the clouds denied them a white Christmas and then dumped a foot of snow the day before Easter.

Sadie rolled down the driver's-side window and called, "Sorry we're late! I had to drive slow on this road; it took longer than I thought it would. We tried to call, but we couldn't get a signal."

"It's fine," Jack said, deeply relieved that his son was there at all. "Thanks for bringing him." Jack had offered to pick Wyatt up, but Sadie had insisted that she could drop him off on the way to the cafe that morning.

"I've got to get to work," Sadie said. "Have fun!"

She looked nervous, and Jack knew that it wasn't about his ability to keep Wyatt safe in the woods... but rather about the likelihood that he could go a full day without pissing the kid off. Well, he couldn't blame her. Jack was worried about that, too.

"Bye, Mom!" Wyatt said cheerfully. He loped over to Jack, daypack slung over one shoulder.

Jack grinned at his son, surprised to find that he had to look *up* at him. The seventeen year old was still growing—and a good inch in the short time he'd been away. He was on track to be the tallest person in the family; already he was level with Gayle's son Reid.

"Where are we headed?" Wyatt asked.

"I thought I'd give you a quick tour of the cabin first," Jack said. The end of the sentence lifted up in a question —*not* a habit that Jack was usually prone to.

"Sure," Wyatt said amiably. They walked up the stairs and into the cabin, where Jack showed him the supplies that were stored there. There were guides of all sorts—edible plants, mushrooms, animal tracks, varieties of trees, birding books, survival guides that detailed how to make fire and shelters, how to purify water, or how to find your way north—plus supplies that they kept on hand for their classes. First aid kits, ropes for learning how to tie knots and hang food, climbing gear, rustic traps, and more.

"Can I borrow this?" Wyatt asked. His dark eyes were wide as he flipped through a particularly comprehensive tome on all-weather survival.

"Of course," Jack replied. He was not in the habit of loaning out these reference books, but the thought of denying his son any aspect of a wilderness education didn't even cross his mind. Who knew—something in that book might save Wyatt's life someday, or the life of one of his friends.

"I have plenty of food," Jack told him, opening a bag of dehydrated meals.

Wyatt gave him a lopsided grin. "Mom took care of that." He opened his backpack to reveal two massive sandwiches and a bag of cookies.

"Of course." Jack faltered. "I have thermoses, too, if you want something hot to drink? I made coffee and, erm, hot chocolate." Offering cocoa to a boy who was taller than he was suddenly seemed absurd, and he hoped that Wyatt wouldn't take offence. But his son just grinned and poured some of each into an empty thermos, then added a heaping tablespoon of sugar.

"It's a mocha," he said. "So, where are we headed?"

"That depends," Jack replied. "What do you want to focus on today?"

Without missing a beat, Wyatt said, "How about how to build a shelter?"

Jack's stomach dropped. How was it that his son was nearly a grown man, and Jack had never taught him to do that? Even River had known how to make a basic shelter before—

No.

Jack took a deep, steadying breath. He wouldn't let himself get mired in guilt. Not today. He would focus on the present moment—inhabit the now, as his grief counselor would say.

Wyatt's smile faltered. "Is that okay?"

Jack forced a grin. "Of course. That's a great place to start. I was just thinking about the best place for us to hike today if that's what we're going to focus on. I know the perfect spot. Let's head out." Jack picked up a full-sized hiking backpack. It was much heavier than anything he would normally use for a day hike, but he wanted to be prepared for anything that Wyatt might like to learn today. There was plenty of water for him and the boy, and a wide range of tools besides—even some lightweight books in case Wyatt wanted to look up plants or mushrooms. Jack didn't mind the added weight; it was good exercise.

They set off into the woods, following a well-worn path for the first couple of hours before they left the path behind and set off through the woods. It was a frigid spring day, and frost crackled beneath their feet. But it was warm enough for a hike, even pleasant once they were a mile in and fully warmed up. Jack spoke every now and again, pointing out markers or birds, stopping to pick bright red partridge-berry fruits and offer some to Wyatt. They were nearly tasteless, but they were one of only two wild plants that offered food in Maine this time of year —the first thaw, whenever that happened. The other was another red berry that grew on a shrub called eastern spicy wintergreen.

"Similar to these, but even smaller," Jack told his son. "Keep an eye out. They're called spiceberry, or teaberry.

They have a minty flavor, so some people like to mash them up and steep them for tea."

As they worked their way up the side of the mountain, Jack was impressed by how quick and agile his son was. They'd hiked a fair number of miles when Wyatt was small, but it was astounding to watch him move with the assurance of a man... a very young man, Jack noted with a grin as Wyatt climbed a boulder just for the fun of it. Between his long legs and lightweight pack, Wyatt was leaping from rock to rock like a mountain goat while Jack walked steadily up the mountainside.

"You're in good shape," Jack said with approval.

The boy flushed a little, clearly pleased. "My school's in the mountains. There's plenty of good hiking around there. I get out a lot. With friends sometimes, or just by myself when I need to clear my head. It helps me stay in shape and get acclimated to the weather. I even hike while I study sometimes."

Jack raised his eyebrows. "How's that?"

"There's an app that will read textbooks to you, like this automated robot voice? But it sounds pretty good, kind of like the narrator on a nature documentary or something. So I download that week's chapters to my phone and listen while I hike. Or I listen to language learning stuff, like this one podcast that helps me with my French. Just with one earbud in," he added with a wry smile. "So I can always be aware of my surroundings." He said this last bit with significance; Jack remembered saying those words to him often when he was a small boy.

They climbed a small peak just for the fun of it and paused there for lunch, taking in the view. Jack pulled a lightweight MRE out of his pack—freeze-dried beef stew—along with a bowl and a thermos of hot water. Wyatt frowned at him and Jack raised his eyebrows.

"What?"

Wyatt chuckled. "Why do you think Mom packed two sandwiches? I eat a lot, but not *that* much." He pulled one of the oversized sandwiches out of his pack and handed it to Jack. It was wrapped in foil, still warm. Sadie had cut a small loaf of fresh-baked sourdough in half and stuffed it with hand-sliced salami, mortadella, and roasted red peppers.

"I know you're not accustomed to eating cafe fare in the woods," Wyatt ribbed him gently. "I promise not to tell anyone and ruin your reputation. I don't think one gourmet sandwich will turn you soft."

"I'll just pretend it's a pile of grubs," Jack replied, deadpan.

Wyatt snorted with laughter, and Jack grinned.

They were quiet for a while, eating the delicious, hearty sandwiches and enjoying the view.

"This might be my favorite place in the state," Jack confided as faraway clouds cleared to reveal the ocean sparkling in the distance. "Though, I don't suppose it compares to the Swiss Alps."

"It's beautiful here, too," Wyatt said. "Just... different."

Jack nearly swallowed the next thing he wanted to say, but then he steeled himself and took a chance. "I would love to visit you out there, while you're still in school. Meet out at the end of the year for a bit of travel, maybe. I've never seen Europe. Or even just a long weekend sometime next winter, a bit of skiing together?"

"I'd like that," Wyatt said, sounding shy. "Either way."

After lunch, they hiked a little ways back down the peak and Jack taught his son how to identify a good campsite and how to make a basic lean-to out of pine boughs. Together, they made quick work of it. After a couple of hours, they had a comfortable shelter that could fit the two of them with room to spare and keep them dry —more or less— even if it rained.

When Jack finally glanced at his watch, it was midafternoon.

"I guess we should be heading back," Wyatt said.

Was Jack imagining things, or did his son sound reluctant to hike back to civilization?

"We need to leave now if you want to get back before dark," Jack acknowledged. "Unless... if you want to do more— maybe look for food sources, learn how to tell if water is good to drink and how to purify it if it isn't—well, we've done all this work. It'll be a cold night, but we *could* put this shelter to use and camp out. I could show you how to build a fire, how to make a rod and find bait... I know a place nearby where we could probably catch some fish for dinner. Make up some pallets to sleep out on pine needles..."

Wyatt's eyes lit up, but his excitement flickered and died as he said, "That sounds like a blast, but I told Mom I'd be home for dinner. My phone doesn't work out here, and I don't want to worry her by staying out all night."

"No," Jack said, "I wouldn't do that to her, either." He pulled a small gadget from his pack, a satellite phone that he always carried in case of emergencies. "You can call her on this, if you'd like."

Wyatt's smile was like the sun coming out. Then, he gave a casual shrug. "Yeah, I guess we could do that. Let me call Mom. I'm sure she'll be fine with it." Wyatt accepted the phone and turned it on... then hesitated and looked up at Jack. "Are you sure you have time? You don't have something else you need to do?"

He did. Jack had classes scheduled the next morning, and Corinne was expecting him for dinner tonight. But none of that mattered; he could make some calls of his own, maybe when he sent the boy out to look for firewood. Jack shook his head, trying to get his emotions in check so that his voice would be steady when he spoke again. It only took him a couple of seconds to reply, but the pause felt long. There was an overabundance of feeling swirling through his chest...

Gratitude. Relief. Grief. Hope.

At last, he said, "There's nothing I'd rather be doing than this, son."

23

GAYLE

It felt good to be pulling together a winning combination of appetizers again, even... no, especially when she was arranging a charcuterie board for her and Kellan.

He had invited her up to the cabin for dinner, and Gayle had offered to bring a bottle of red wine and one of her famous charcuterie boards. Her favorite little grocery store—one in downtown Cherry Blossom Point that specialized in gourmet foods—had everything that she needed. Her favorite cherry-wood board was in the car, and assembling the food once she arrived would be quick work.

Gayle pulled up to Kellan's house right on time, and she was surprised to see an unfamiliar car parked in front of the cabin.

She climbed cautiously out of her car to see two women sitting on the porch swing, one with white hair and one with gray.

"Hello!" called the older woman, waving. "You must be Gayle!"

A vague feeling of dread washed over Gayle as she waved back. She supposed she should say something in reply, but the words stuck in her throat. She circled around to her trunk to grab her charcuterie board and two bags of groceries.

"Dinner's nearly ready," the white-haired woman said as Gayle walked towards them. Gayle recognized her now, just as a face that she often saw around town. "Kellan kicked us out of the kitchen. You know how he gets when he's cooking."

Did she? Gayle swallowed and walked up the front steps.

The younger woman jumped to her feet. "Your hands are full. Let me get the door."

Up close, the woman was stunning. Even her hair, dull gray from a distance, was beautiful...waves of gray-black highlighted with strands of silver. She was young, maybe forty, with beautiful hazel green eyes.

"I'm Christy," the woman confided when Gayle met her gaze.

"Oh, I think she knows who we are," Mrs. Hayes chortled.

"I'm Kellan's little sister," Christy added, confirming what Gayle, indeed, already knew.

Kellan had decided to use this dinner to introduce her to his family.

"Pleased to meet you," Gayle managed. The truth was, she didn't feel pleased. She felt ambushed and terrified.

"It's good to meet you, too." Christy's smile was charming, but Gayle felt slightly sick to her stomach. She walked through the open door and set her bags down on the kitchen counter. Kellan hardly glanced up.

"Hello," he greeted her. "I have potatoes roasting and I'm pan-frying the steaks now. Dinner will be ready soon."

"I brought some things," Gayle said weakly.

"Great."

Kellan had his back to her, and Gayle's hands shook as she began emptying her grocery bags. So much for a romantic dinner date. Gayle set a jar of fig jam on the counter with a *thwack*. Kellan didn't so much as flinch.

"Can I help with anything?" Christy asked. She came through the front door and hung her coat on a peg that Gayle had never noticed before; she'd left her own coat draped over the back of the couch.

Gayle shrugged and tried to let go of the senseless terror that was making it difficult for her to function.

What was the big deal? It wasn't like a marriage proposal or something. She'd managed to get a handle on her control issues with her siblings. Surely, she could do the same with Kellan?

This was fine, she reassured herself. Everything was great.

"Would you like a glass of red wine?" she found herself asking the other woman in a shrill voice.

Christy smiled. "Sure." She paused, catching sight of the items on the counter. "Are you making a charcuterie board?"

Gayle nodded. "I am."

"Oh, what a treat!" Christy pulled a corkscrew from a drawer and opened the bottle of wine as she spoke. "Your charcuterie boards are the best I've ever had. I used to get them at The Milky Thistle."

Gayle frowned. She knew all of her regulars by name, and Christy wasn't one of them.

Christy seemed to read Gayle's thoughts. "It's been a long time," she admitted. "Back when you first opened. I moved down to Portland when I got married, and I haven't been home much. Until recently." A shadow of stress and sorrow passed over Christy's face, but she pressed on. "Kellan told us that you and your business partner are opening a brand new restaurant and bar?"

"That's right." Gayle cut a block of caramelized onion cheddar into careful, even slices.

"And you'll have axe throwing there? It sounds like so much fun!"

Gayle smiled, charmed by Christy's enthusiasm, in spite of herself. "It'll be different from The Milky Thistle, that's for sure. We're going for a rustic theme, right down to wooden trenchers and handmade cutlery. Beer in steins, that sort of thing. But a nicer dining area up top, too, to bring in older couples for date nights and families for weekend brunch. The plan is to offer lots of wild game and foraged foods—we're calling it Hunter's Gathering—but the menu isn't even close to figured out." She thought of Nikki and smiled. "I think we've secured an amazing chef, though."

"I'm so excited to see what you do with the place!" Christy stole a slice of salami as Gayle put her finishing touches on the board.

Gayle chuckled self-consciously as she crafted a bite-sized tower of fig jam, prosciutto, and Manchego atop a cracker.

"Me too," she told Christy, and took a bite.

"Dinner's ready," Kellan said, and Gayle shot him a glance.

He was usually so slow and methodical with things, so

rushing past the cheese board felt off, somehow. They were just supposed to eat it with venison and potatoes?

Gayle shrugged and ate a dried apricot from the platter.

"Mom insists on eating early," Christy murmured in a low voice. "We'll be out of your hair well before eight—she usually goes to bed around then. She is *spry* for seventy-seven, but she gets tired in the evenings."

"It's fine." Gayle smiled and shot a glance at Kellan, but he had his back to her again, pulling a tray of crispy potatoes from the oven.

The door opened and Mrs. Hayes walked in. She, too, hung her coat on a near-invisible wooden peg by the front door.

"Is dinner ready yet?" she demanded.

"Fresh out of the oven," Christy said, sparing a surreptitious wink at Gayle.

The older woman hopped easily up onto one of the stools that served as Kellan's dining chairs. Gayle settled across from the other women, sitting on the kitchen side of the butcher-block counter. She took one last little bite of food from the charcuterie platter as Kellan set a hearty portion of venison and potatoes down in front of her.

"There's sauerkraut, too," he offered, setting a jar of greenish-white cabbage in the middle of the table. It smelled like pickles, the kind that Gayle's grandmother used to make. She realized, suddenly, that she'd never tried the preserves Kellan had sent her home with the first time she'd been here. Nikki had used the eggs, but the jars of vegetables had been lost to the chaotic overabundance of food that was constantly cycling through Nikki's kitchen.

She took a long drink of her wine as Kellan sat down next

to her.

"This wine is delicious, Gayle," he said as he took a sip. He squeezed her leg under the table, and her nerves calmed some.

"How about those pickles you make, son?" said Mrs. Hayes.

"I don't have any jars open," Kellan replied, "but there's more in the root cellar."

"Would you?"

"Let him eat, Mom," Christy protested.

"No, it's fine," Kellan said. "You all go ahead and eat. I'll be right back."

"So, Gayle," Mrs. Hayes said the moment Kellan was out the door. "You have two grown children, is that right? And you're divorced?"

Gayle just nodded, caught with a mouthful of venison.

"And do they live in town?" asked Mrs. Hayes.

"Out of state."

"Why is that, I wonder?" the old woman asked intently, leaning forward to peer at Gayle.

Gayle shook her head and forked up another bite of food. It was delicious, but her enjoyment was tempered by the fact that she was being grilled even harder than the meat in front of her.

"They left for college," Gayle faltered, feeling her cheeks color, "and their careers..."

"Mother," Christy protested, "stop that!"

Mrs. Hayes paid her no mind. "It's such a shame that young people today are so career focused, even the women. They don't understand what's really important."

"Mom," Christy groaned.

"Now, it's not your fault, dear, but really. Look at what all those feminists and college professors put in your heads, telling you that you can have it all. Well, I'm sorry they lied to you, because you quite simply cannot have it all. There are only so many hours in a day, so many years in a lifetime. Look at Christy, for example." Mrs. Hayes turned back to Gayle as her daughter stared at her in horror. "Put her career first, always figuring she would have time for family later. Didn't get married until well into her thirties. Well, here she is, forty-two and separated—"

"Mom, *stop*," Christy pleaded.

"I did the opposite," Gayle confided, feeling terrible for the lovely woman across from her. "I prioritized my children and tried to keep my marriage together way past its expiration date. Didn't start my career until I was your age. And look where it got me. Kids in another state, my bar being run into the ground by my ex-husband... There's just no knowing how life will turn out. Don't you think?"

Kellan came back in then, and his mother gave him a beatific smile.

"Ah, your famous pickles! Thank you, my dear."

"No problem," Kellan said easily. He opened the jar, sat down, and tucked into his food. The table was silent for a while, each of them working away at their amazingly tender venison steaks. Kellan didn't seem to mind the silence in the least, but Christy looked as miserably uncomfortable as Gayle felt.

"So, um, what do you do for a living, Christy?" she asked.

Christy smiled self-consciously and tucked a strand of silver hair behind her ear. "Well, two things. I'm a poet—"

"A *published* poet," Mrs. Hayes added.

"—but that doesn't exactly pay the bills. So I do graphic design, as well. I worked for a company down in Portland, but just this year I've switched over to freelance work, running my own business. The transition was a headache, but day to day I like it a lot better. Being able to set my own hours and pick and choose the clients I want to work with. I'm really enjoying it."

"That's fascinating," Gayle replied. "What sort of work do you do?"

"Anything, really. I kind of got hemmed into ads when I was working in Portland, and I was so tired of that sort of work. I still do that a bit, but I've been branching out, too. It keeps things interesting. I really like working with text, and I've had so much experience with that in my own work. I do books of poetry, but other stuff, too. Text in the shape of pictures, that sort of thing."

"I wonder if you could help us with the branding for our restaurant?" Gayle asked. "We haven't found anyone to design the menus yet, and we could use help with our logo and everything."

"Yeah, I would love that. If you give me your email, I could send over my portfolio?"

Gayle pulled a business card from her purse. It still had The Milky Thistle's name and logo on it, and she gave Christy a look somewhere between a grin and a grimace. "As you can see, I need new business cards, too."

Christy grinned in reply. "I can help with that."

Mrs. Hayes was on her best behavior all through the rest of dinner, but Gayle still felt on edge pretty much the whole time. She'd shown up for what she expected to be a relaxing, romantic date with Kellan Hayes... and instead she walked into what felt like a trap and found herself being interviewed by his mother.

How could he not warn her? If he *had* asked, she would have demurred. It was too soon for this, much too soon. Sure, he already knew some of her family, but that was different. She wasn't ready to introduce him to her father, certainly wasn't ready to so much as mention his name to her kids. She and Kellan had only been out together a couple of times. This was a huge jump forward in their relationship that Gayle wasn't ready for.

She had just gotten out of a terrible marriage. The ink was barely dry on the divorce paperwork. Her kids had only just forgiven her. This was happening way too fast. She was preparing to launch a brand new restaurant. She didn't have time for any of this. She liked Kellan—liked him a lot.

But for someone who usually moseyed his way through life, he was scaring the crap out of her with this breakneck race into a serious relationship.

"So, Gayle," Mrs. Hayes began as she pushed away her empty dinner plate. Gayle was only halfway through her meal; she didn't have much of an appetite. Her single glass of wine was long-since gone, though. "What is it that you like to do for fun, when you're not working seventy hours a week at this new restaurant of yours?"

"I don't have much time for fun."

And she had zero patience for another round of twenty loaded questions with Kellan's mother.

She set her fork and knife down and took a deep breath as she slipped off her stool to stand on the kitchen floor.

"And on that note, I just remembered that I have to contact the plumber about an issue at the restaurant. I'm so sorry to cut this short..." She turned away from Mrs. Hayes and offered Christy a tired smile. "It was so nice meeting you both, but duty calls."

"I understand. Priorities are priorities, dear," Kellan's mother said with a pointed glance at her son.

Gayle grabbed her purse and coat and managed a finger wiggle at them before heading to the door.

"I'll walk you out," Kellan said as he stood and trailed behind her.

Once they were outside, he reached for her hand.

"Hey...Are you okay? I know my mother can be a lot, but-"

"I'm good. Totally fine," she cut in, the torrent of emotions stuck in her chest. "I'm just tired."

Well, she was.

"And I have a big day tomorrow."

She did.

But that wasn't the reason she was leaving...and she was pretty sure by the stricken look on Kellan's face as she turned away and scurried to her car, he knew it.

As she put the car into drive, she squashed back the guilt and disappointment.

What was the big deal? They'd spent a little time together, and now, it was over.

So what if she'd gotten more pleasure out of fishing with Kellan than she'd gotten in the past ten years with Rex?

So what if he brought out a new side of her that made her see the world in a different light?

So what if he'd given her hope that she could eat her cake and have it, too?

So freaking what?

24

NIKKI

"You are *terrible* at this," Beth crowed, laughing.

"Well, excuse me if I have better things to do than play video games all day." Wyatt's tone was cheerful. "Try me on a real mountain and we'll see who wins."

Nikki smiled and shook her head. Life as an only child could be lonely, but having a cousin in town was just as good. Better, sometimes—all the fun of a sibling without the inevitable fighting that came from living in the same house. Beth was only a year older than Wyatt, and they'd been thick as thieves ever since Nikki and Beth had moved home to Cherry Blossom Point... well over a decade ago now. With Beth away at college and Wyatt living in Switzerland, they hardly saw each other anymore. Beth had been sorry to miss Kiera the month before, but delighted to discover that her spring break overlapped with her cousin's.

She turned back to Gayle, who was looking over a handwritten mockup of the opening menu for Hunter's Gathering. Or... she was supposed to be. When Nikki looked closer, she realized that her sister's eyes were staring into middle distance, not quite focused on the paper in front of her.

"Gayle?" she prompted.

"Yeah?" Gayle blinked, seeming to come back into her body. She looked down at the menu. "What were you thinking for the wild game sausages? What ingredients, I mean?"

"That's just one way to give us wiggle room so we can use a consistent menu for the bar," Nikki replied. "It would be weekly specials depending on what we have in stock. Venison, rabbit, whatever. I'll probably have to doctor them with local pork to get the fat content right... game meat is pretty dry."

"How would we serve them?"

"We could get some good buns and serve them like gourmet hotdogs with homemade toppings. Or it could be a more immersive experience... like precooked sausages for people to warm over the fire. Depending on whether they're upstairs or down in the bar."

Gayle grinned. "I like it."

"And then I wrote down some other staples to round out the menu, because it can't be all game all the time. Poutine would be a fun one, and we could stay on brand with a gravy made from some kind of wild game. Local eggs, for sure, and not just for the weekend brunch—I'm thinking some kind of warm salad dish with a poached egg on top. We'll use foraged ingredients when we can. See the fiddlehead fern dish I have there, near the top?"

"Yeah. Sounds good."

"What do you think of the moose burgers?"

"Definitely," Gayle said.

"Those will need bacon, too, either mixed into the burgers or on top. It's just so lean... or if we don't want to do bacon, I could default to cheeseburgers. Some kind of extra ooey gooey cheese. Or an aioli—that might work best, because we can incorporate locally foraged ingredients and make something really unique."

"Yep, sounds good."

Nikki frowned at her sister. Was she imagining things, or was Gayle not all here today? She rifled through her notes for the dessert menu and set it down in front of Gayle.

"I was thinking of kind of the same thing with desserts. We can do some crowd-pleasers like chocolate lava cake, but kind of keep on theme by topping them with dried elderflowers, wild berry compote, that kind of thing. In the summertime, we can get a bit more creative... a tart made from wild blueberries, maybe, or elderberry cheesecake. Maybe elderflower fritters. Have you ever heard of deep-fried maple leaves?"

"Yeah, good." Gayle's eyes were on the menu, but her mind was somewhere else entirely. Nikki bristled inwardly. She was putting her whole heart into this, and her sister wasn't even paying attention. She was about to say something when Beth and Wyatt walked in.

"Did you say fried maple leaves?" Beth asked, pulling half of a chocolate cake out of the fridge.

Nikki grinned at her. "Yeah. You can pick them in summertime and pack them in salt, and they'll stay good for nearly a year. Then you can just pull them out as needed."

"That's crazy," she said with approval. "What about that pine cake you were talking about?"

"Yeah, I think that would be a great fit for Hunter's Gathering." Nikki looked over at Gayle. "It's this rich, dense cake with brown sugar and ground-up pine needles. Really unique."

Wyatt opened the fridge and pulled out a glass jar of milk. "That sounds bomb. Any chance you could make that for Easter? You know, just to test it out?"

Beth didn't look at all like her reedy cousin, but her devilish grin was just the same. "Quality control, right, Mom?"

Nikki laughed. "I just might."

The kids walked out, and Nikki turned back to her sister. "What do you think?"

"Yeah, sounds great."

Nikki's eyes narrowed. "I figured we'd do a possum pudding, too, with a side of skunk cabbage. And some gravel on top, for crunch."

Gayle nodded, still looking down at the papers in front of her. "Yeah, for crunch. Sounds good."

Nikki slapped her hand on the marble countertop, and Gayle looked up with a start.

"What is *with* you today?" Nikki demanded. "I know you have a lot on your plate, but the menu is important. I wanted to get the green light before I narrow it down and work on perfecting the recipes, but you're not even paying attention. So, let's hear it. What's going on with you?"

"It's nothing," Gayle said, eyes darting to one side.

"No." Nikki held up both hands and waved them back and forth. "I'm not having it. The Axis of Evil protecting the young'uns from their pain is *so* last season. Is it Rex? The Milky Thistle? What?"

Gayle groaned and rested her forehead on the countertop. A moment later, she was on her feet, pacing back and forth within the confines of Nikki's kitchen.

"I'm sorry. You're right, of course the menu is important. I just can't stop thinking about Kellan Hayes."

Nikki laughed in surprise. Here she was thinking that Gayle was in crisis, when really she was just gaga over a hot guy. "The mountain man?"

Gayle's pacing didn't pause, but she met Nikki's eyes and nodded. Another groan. "He swept me off my feet, Nikki, and then I bolted like some sort of lunatic. I literally just ran out of his house with some lame excuse instead of, you know, talking to him like a grown up."

"Back up," Nikki said. "He *swept you off your feet*?"

She had never known her sister not to have both feet solidly planted on the ground. Even when she had married Rex, she'd been remarkably calm and level-headed about it all. Nikki had been so young, but it had occurred to her even then that Gayle had seen marriage more as a path to children and family than something to embark on solely out of love for the man himself. It certainly hadn't satisfied Nikki's teenage dreams of what a happily ever after should look like. Gayle had loved Rex, sure, but always in a good-enough kind of way. At least, that was how Nikki remembered it. It wasn't as if Gayle had shared her truest, deepest feelings with her kid sister. Not then, at least.

Gayle slumped back onto one of the barstools and took a sip of her tea. "First, he invited me axe throwing. He introduced me to his animals and told me that I *smelled* good. Then, he took me fly fishing. I *know*!" she said in response to the look on Nikki's face. "But I *loved* it! I mean, I hated it. At first. And then he reminded me to look around, and *breathe*, and next thing I knew it was sunset. He cooked up the fish he'd caught and then he... he kissed me. Nikki, I don't know if I've ever felt this way about anyone. I don't have *time* for this."

Nikki held her tongue and the smile that pulled at her lips, giving her sister the space to keep talking.

"Then, he took me out on a real date. Dinner at La Traviata. And afterwards, he drove us up out of town and spread out this blanket—don't look at me like that!" she interrupted herself, cheeks coloring. "He threw down this quilt and we watched the most spectacular meteor shower. I can't remember the last time I stopped and looked up at the stars. He has this knack for getting me to slow down."

"Wow," Nikki said. That was no small feat.

"I know." Gayle put her face in her hands.

"So... what's the problem? Why did you bolt?"

"I showed up for a dinner date—just, what, our third date? I don't think the axe throwing counts... Anyway, I show up at the cabin and who's sitting on the front porch but his *mother* and his little sister. I felt completely ambushed. I left before dessert and I haven't seen him since."

"Has he called?" Nikki asked.

"Every day. Once a day. I haven't called him back."

"Poor guy," Nikki murmured.

Gayle groaned again. "I know. But I have no idea what to say to him. And honestly? I really miss him. His work at the bar is done... I feel torn, Nikki. I miss the anticipation of seeing him, but it's all so overwhelming. It's too much too fast."

"What are you scared of?"

"What if it doesn't work out?" Gayle said immediately. "What if those endearing traits of being so calm and easygoing is just a precursor to him lying around the house all day like Rex, with no motivation at all?" She scrunched up her nose at her own questions, as if she knew they were absurd, but she couldn't stop worrying about them. "What if... what if I'm looking for stupid reasons to pull away because I'm terrified of giving him my whole heart just so he can break it?"

Nikki let out a low whistle as she reached across the counter and took Gayle's hand. "That's deep, introspective stuff, sister mine."

They were silent for a long moment, and then Nikki continued.

"I'm sort of in the same boat, you know."

Gayle looked up at her. "How's that?"

"I've been wrestling with what to do about Mateo."

"I thought he was perfect for you."

"As perfect as Kellan?" Nikki shot back.

Gayle flinched and withdrew her hand.

"Sorry." Nikki sighed. "He lives two hours away, Gayle. Before you offered me a job at Hunter's Gathering, he asked me to move in with him. He doesn't want to do long distance anymore."

Her sister's eyes widened. "Oh. Oof."

"Oof, indeed," Nikki shot back. "I just wasn't ready. I don't want to move away from Dad or give up my home. I don't want to turn my whole life upside-down for a man that I just met a few months ago. But the way we left things, I don't know what we'll do... I don't know if he even wants to *be* with me if it means staying in a long-distance relationship."

"Two hours isn't that far," Gayle protested.

"It's far enough. I hardly saw him when I was busy with the-restaurant-that-shall-not-be-named... and I'll be just as busy with Hunter's Gathering going forward. And I *want* to be, that's the thing. Beth *just* left for college. I'm ready to focus on *myself*, on my career... but Mateo is wonderful, Gayle. I don't want to lose him. I don't know what to do."

"That's a tough one," Gayle acknowledged. "You know... if moving to Bluebird Bay is what would make you happy, we could still find someone else for Hunter's Gathering."

"But I *want* this job," Nikki said. "I don't want to leave Cherry Blossom Point, at least, not yet. And that's what I have to tell Mateo. I've just been pushing it off... Easter's in a few days, and then Beth goes back to school... I thought I would figure things out then."

"Is he willing to move to Cherry Blossom Point?"

"That's the crazy thing," Nikki admitted. "He is. And even *that* terrifies me. It doesn't make any sense. I guess it feels a little too much like giving up my independence at this point. The last time I did that, I ended up under Steve's thumb to the point that I nearly suffocated."

"Mateo isn't Steve," Gayle said gently. "You can't paint Mateo with the same brush when he hasn't given you any indication that he's like that."

Nikki nodded as she looked back at Gayle with an exaggerated tilt of her head. "Same goes for Kellan...right? Rex was lazy, Kellan is clearly not that. He's the polar opposite of lazy. Look how fast he finished that project at the new bar. And what has he ever done to make you think he'd cheat or break your heart?"

Gayle looked down. "Yeah, I suppose that's true."

Nikki gave her a wry smile. "Why is it that other people's problems are always so much clearer than our own?"

"Damned if I know," Gayle said with a laugh.

"Mateo and I want the same thing," Nikki said, thinking aloud. "I do enjoy spending time with him. I would love to see him more often. And right now, I think the only way to make that work is for him to move. I won't leave my family now, and I want this job. We just need to sit down and hash it out. But I feel so selfish asking Mateo to leave his life and the house that he *just* remodeled..."

"He's a grown man. He has a choice, just like you do. You just have to believe you're worth the compromise for him."

"Yeah," Nikki said with a sigh. She knew Gayle was right. "And what about you? Can you at least talk to Kellan and see if maybe you're worth the compromise, too? Tell him you need to take it slow? Ghosting him like this is just wrong. He probably doesn't even know what he did to deserve it."

Gayle winced. "You're right. He did nothing to deserve it at all. I wasn't happy about the surprise family introduction, and instead of talking it through, I got spooked. This thing with Rex has just been a lot..." She seemed to come to a decision, and stood so quickly that her stool rattled in protest. "I'm going to go talk to him. Can we get back to the menu later? Tomorrow, maybe?"

"Of course," Nikki said. "Go."

Gayle pulled her into a quick hug and strode out, looking determined. Nikki could hear the kids in the distance; they were playing games on the computer in Beth's room.

It was time to take her own advice.

Trembling slightly with nerves, she picked up her phone and called Mateo.

"Hey," she said when he picked up. "Do you have time to talk?"

25

GAYLE

This wasn't a conversation to be had over the phone. Gayle drove straight to Kellan's house through the pouring rain, buzzing with nerves.

Had she ruined things with him already by ignoring his calls? By "ghosting" him like some college kid? How could she have been so inconsiderate?

But Kellan was a patient man, and it hadn't been *that* long. He would understand... right?

Gayle was relieved to see Kellan's truck —and only Kellan's truck— parked in front of his cabin. She pulled her coat over her head and ran up his front path, wincing as a gust of wind drove icy drops of rain into her face. She made a racket running up the stairs, and Kellan opened the door just as she raised her fist to knock. He stared down at her, surprise visible on his face.

"Gayle." He gave her a slow, slightly confused nod.

"Hi." She let her hand drop. Wind blew across the porch, and she shivered. "Can I come in?"

"Of course." Kellan stepped aside and closed the door behind her as she entered. Gayle hung her coat on the peg by the door and then gravitated towards the heat of the stove. Her hands steamed slightly as she held them out. Kellan handed her a clean towel, which she used to wipe the rainwater from her face and hair. He watched her quietly, and Gayle felt a spasm of guilt when she met his eyes.

"I'm sorry I haven't called you back," she blurted.

His gaze didn't waver. "Would you like to sit down?"

Gayle shook her head.

"I was worried that something happened to you," Kellan said quietly. "But I asked Jack and he said you were alive, so I figured you just... didn't feel like talking."

Gayle brought her fire-warmed hands together, twisting them as she tried to find the right words to explain. She hated that she'd worried him.

He deserved better.

"I got scared," she blurted at last. "I just got out of a long marriage, and I never expected to meet anyone so soon. I was ready to put everything I had into this new business. And honestly, I was terrified. I couldn't believe I was falling for somebody I'd only just met. It was all moving too fast for me, Kellan."

His expression softened. "We can go as slow as you'd like."

"Are you sure?"

"Patience is easy for me, Gayle."

Slowly, Kellan closed the space between them. His strong fingertips rested lightly on her cheek as he bent to kiss her. His eyes were warm with affection and amusement when he pulled back to look at her.

"Life isn't a race to the finish line. You gotta enjoy the trip."

Gayle grinned at him, but she could feel her smile waver as she said, "When you invited your mom and sister over for dinner, I thought that was your way of moving the relationship along. Getting serious."

Kellan took a step back. "You thought I invited them?"

She blinked up at him. "You didn't?"

"Without even telling you?" Kellan shook his head and chuckled. "No, ma'am. They just stopped by. They do that sometimes."

"Oh," Gayle said softly. As if she didn't already feel like a heel...

"And don't worry. My mom can be overbearing, but I have no problem putting her in her place. In fact, I did so the second you left." Kellan's expression turned serious as he said, "You could have just asked me what they were doing here, and I would have explained. I never would have thought you'd take it that way. I was as annoyed as you were that they hijacked our date. I only let them stay because you were due to arrive any minute, and I didn't want to make a big production. I explained to them both that they need to call ahead next time in case we had plans. Although, I hadn't realized you'd planned to ignore my calls at that point..."

Gayle's cheeks grew warm with embarrassment.

"I was an idiot. My love life hasn't exactly been stellar the past... well, ever. I don't know how to do this. I don't know the rules."

Kellan reached for Gayle's hand and gently pulled her towards him.

"You know the best thing about finding a person you

really connect with after fifty?" His voice was low as he pulled Gayle's hand to his chest. Her other hand came up automatically, fingers running over the soft wool of his sweater.

"What's that?" she asked.

"We don't need to follow any rules. We can do whatever we want. And what *I* want is to spend my time getting to know everything about you. What makes you laugh, what makes you cry..." Kellan ran his thumb lightly along Gayle's jaw, and she shivered. He smiled and added, "...what makes you shiver." He touched her lips lightly with one finger, and then bent to kiss her.

Some time later, when they came up for air, Gayle told him, "I want that, too. So much."

EPILOGUE

Gemma sat on a cold plastic table in an exam room at the local clinic, feeling completely dissociated from reality. She could hardly stand to be in her own body anymore. Her life was a waking nightmare. It had been ever since that awful moment when she'd watched an eighteen-wheeler plow into her husband's truck. Before being thrown into shock and grief, she might have assumed that it was something she could overcome quickly... just shake it off. Or at least *pretend* that she was still functioning normally. She would never stop missing her parents, and losing them had torn a hole in her heart... but she had cried and grieved and then picked herself up and kept going.

Now?

She could hardly get through a day, could hardly remember who she was anymore. Liam and Aiden kept her grounded, but just barely.

She was failing them.

A responsible mother would have made this appointment

months ago, would have made *sure* to stay on top of her health for the sake of her children. But Gemma had hardly given her symptoms any attention. The lack of appetite, constant nausea, chronic exhaustion... she'd chalked it all up to losing the love of her life before either of them had turned forty. Grief could do this to a person, she knew that. Stress took a terrible toll on the body.

She'd experienced it herself when her mother died. Gemma had been diagnosed with Hashimoto's thyroiditis after Aiden was born, but she'd wrestled the autoimmune disease into submission with the help of a functional medicine doctor in Denver. When she ate well and took the supplements her doctor recommended, Gemma usually felt fine. But after her mother's death, the symptoms that she normally kept in remission had flared back to life. She was tired all the time. Her joints hurt. Hell, her *bones* hurt. It had all subsided eventually, after a few doctor's visits and deliberate self-care.

So when she grew ill following Jerry's death, she assumed it was the same. Especially when she forgot to take her supplements for days at a time, or forgot to order them in time and had to wait for them to arrive from Denver. She was so upset in the weeks following the accident that she could hardly keep a piece of toast down, much less eat the types of balanced meals that kept her healthy. She'd lost so much weight that she had to use one of Jerry's old belts to keep her pants from falling down. When she was coherent enough to wonder about it, she kept putting it off to grief.

But she couldn't deny it any longer. It had been too long. Gemma was sick, and not with the same old autoimmune issues that she knew how to manage.

If she died, Liam and Aiden would be orphans. She knew that Owen and Lena would step in, but she could only imagine how deeply affected the boys would be by the loss of *both* their parents. Hell, losing her mother as an *adult* had been devastating. Losing them both so young would be awful for the boys.

Gemma took a deep breath and let it out slowly, trying to calm her frantically beating heart.

This wouldn't do her a bit of good. She was putting the cart before the horse. It was stress, that was all. New autoimmune symptoms, some mineral deficiency, something she could *fix*.

"Sorry to keep you waiting!" The doctor rushed in, closing the door behind her. "I'm Dr. Singh. You can call me Mira."

Gemma's voice caught in her throat, but she managed a smile.

"Your bloodwork all looks fine," Mira said, settling onto a stool as she opened Gemma's file, "but I understand you've been feeling poorly? Your vitamin D is a bit low, and you may find that higher doses of B6 can help to prevent the nausea you've been experiencing. I see you left the date of your last period blank? We'll need that for our records."

Gemma thought back. It had been months, but she hadn't given that much thought. Oligomenorrhea was a common symptom of Hashimoto's; it was the primary symptom that had sent her in search of help years ago, what had helped her to finally get a diagnosis for the debilitating fatigue she'd experienced when her boys were small. Of course it had come back with this latest flare up. But it had been a long time... not since Denver.

"I don't know the exact date," she told the doctor. "Late November, I guess? Somewhere in there."

"Okay, so that would give us a due date of..." Mira paused, then said, "late August? If you have any journals or records that you could look through for a date, that would help. Sometimes thinking about past trips or things like that can trigger a reminder. Have you been taking any prenatal vitamins?"

Gemma's vision shrunk to a pinprick, and there was a roaring in her ears. She may have blacked out for a minute, because when she became aware of Mira again, the doctor's face was filled with concern.

"Gemma? Are you alright?"

She shook her head. "I'm not. I can't be."

Mira closed the file and stared at Gemma in shock. "I am so sorry, Gemma. Did you not know that you were pregnant? You... you're entering your second trimester."

The room seemed to spin as Gemma fought for breath.

"O- ol- oligomenorrhea," she managed.

Mira opened the file again and flipped back to the pages that had been faxed over from Denver.

"Oh," she said. "Oh, I see. No, Gemma. I'm so sorry for the miscommunication. I should have— No, your bloodwork shows that you're pregnant. And it says here that your menses had been pretty regular for a few years before you conceived? I can see why your mind went there, if you have a history of... but no, Gemma. We can schedule an ultrasound right away, to get a better idea of how far along—"

She kept talking, but Gemma didn't register the rest. She was suddenly flooded with memories of Jerry. She could see him so clearly in her mind's eye, that nineteen-year-old boy with a dazzling grin. They had met playing Ultimate, and he was always snatching the frisbee away a microsecond before Gemma could catch it. It had infuriated her... until he had switched over to her team, just to spend more time with Gemma.

She remembered Jerry at twenty-six, so incredibly handsome in the untucked collared shirt he'd worn on their wedding day... outside in the sunshine, a quiet ceremony by the lakeside.

She could still see the expression on his face when he took Liam into his arms for the first time.

His bloodied face as he took his last breath, eyes locked on hers...

The father of her children.

Everything had seemed so stressful the year before, when he got laid off from his job. Jerry had been depressed, and Gemma was overwhelmed. But he had been so supportive when she'd been offered that job in Boston. They'd been excited for the fresh start, and things seemed to be getting better. They'd had such high hopes for the future. And now?

Gemma's hand went to her belly.

Jerry had given her one final gift... and she had no idea how she would find the strength to handle it.

Did you enjoy A Fresh Start? Check out Gemma's story, A Head Start, coming November of 2021!

Gemma McKenna has finally come to grips with her husband's death but is reeling once again when she realizes that he left her a final gift. Already overwhelmed by the thought of raising their two sons alone, finding out that she has a baby on the way nearly sends her over the edge. She has her brother Owen and her friends in Cherry Blossom Point to lean on, but they have their own lives and responsibilities. When she meets her handsome neighbor, Patrick, and his sweet daughter, Zoe, she is relieved to find another single parent to bond with. But when their friendship starts to feel like something more, she can't help but feel like she's committing the ultimate betrayal...

Gayle Merrill has been forced to reinvent herself in a lot of ways over the past year, and it's been great...mostly. She's got a new man, a better relationship with her siblings, and a fresh outlook on life. But she never imagined that leaving her miserable marriage would cost her the business she's worked so hard for. Now, with no choice but to pull herself up by her bootstraps and start again, she'll see what she's truly made of. She created a successful business once. Can she do it again, or is catching lightning in a bottle twice in one lifetime too much to ask?

Jack Merrill isn't perfect, but dang if he isn't trying to be a better man...and a better father. In the past, he'd been so broken inside, he'd allowed his relationship with his son to crumble right before his very eyes. But now that he and his true love, Corinne, are back together, he feels invincible. This former soldier is ready to fight to get Wyatt back in his life, and he won't stop until the battle is won.

Gemma

. . .

"One more load...maybe two," Owen said with a quick, easy grin as he set down a box marked "kitchen" and made for the door. "Then, the hard work is done."

God, how she wished that were true.

But Gemma managed a smile for her brother before he jogged back outside to the moving truck.

He and Lena, his long-time best friend and relatively new beloved, had been such a big help to her and the boys these past months, ever since her life had gotten turned upside down. When they'd left Denver just before the holidays and returned to New England, Gemma and her little family had been ready to turn the page and start a new chapter. She never could have guessed that this new chapter would start with her husband's death.

After losing Jerry to a head-on collision, Gemma had done her best to hold it together for her two boys, Liam and Aiden. She had stuffed her grief into a little box, started at her new job only a couple weeks later than she'd planned, and did her best to move on with life. Despite her best efforts, though, everything had slowly crumbled around...and within her. She'd lost the job-- nearly lost her mind-- when her brother had come to her house and practically dragged her back home to Cherry Blossom Point where he could help.

For the first few months, they'd stayed at his girlfriend Lena's place, and now she and her boys were finally moving into a place of their own. After being in limbo for so long, it felt like a homecoming. And in many ways, it was.

Gemma had been five when her family moved into this house, and she'd lived there until she left for college at seventeen. Even then, the house had served as her home base for years. Every Christmas, she'd come home to spend the holidays with her family. She'd come home most Easters as well, and every summer she'd managed to visit for at least a week or two.

Until their mother died.

Jerry had carried her through that. Her husband hadn't always been able to anchor her--he struggled with anxiety and depression that had left him incapacitated some days-- but during that last trip to her childhood home, he had been her rock.

While she and Owen had been too mired in grief to deal with everything that kept coming at them--the memorial service, obituary, paperwork, unpaid bills--they had left the rest to Jerry. He'd kept precious keepsakes to the side, boxed up the rest of house besides the furniture -- kitchenware, clothes, their dad's old things that still filled the garage -- and donated it all to charity. It was a massive job to accomplish in the time that they were there. But Jerry had handled it without complaint, all while caring for their two little boys. He had even found tenants for the place before they flew back to Colorado.

That quiet couple had stayed in the house until a couple months back, when Owen had let them know that they wouldn't be offering a lease renewal for the year. They'd been very understanding, and now the house was hers. Mortgage free, bought and paid for. One last, enormous gift from her mom and dad. Eventually, she would broach the subject of ensuring Owen got a share in some form or another, but for now, he'd insisted the house was hers, and she was too exhausted and relieved to argue. This gift, plus the money that remained from Jerry's small life insurance policy would see them through for a while yet; not having to pay rent was a huge relief. And, even better, her family home was almost exactly as she remembered it. It was deeply comforting to stand on floors that her father had put down himself, surrounded by the furniture that her mother had chosen.

Gemma paused by the glass-topped dining table, mind casting back to the countless family meals it had held. As her mind wandered, her hand rested on the gentle curve of her stomach.

Less than five months.

Gemma had less than five months before the new baby arrived -- and that was if she made it to term.

And she still hadn't told a soul.

It wasn't that she wanted to keep her pregnancy a secret this whole time. She had been unconscious of it for months, attributing all of her early pregnancy symptoms to grief and illness. It hadn't been the first time she'd missed a period when under stress. And the other signs-- the exhaustion, the lack of appetite-- didn't raise any red flags, given the circumstances. She'd been utterly overwhelmed by Jerry's sudden death, hardly in her right mind.

But she'd known for weeks, now, and still hadn't been able to bring herself to speak the truth aloud. She was already sick to death of seeing the pity in everyone's faces every time they looked at her. On the rare occasion that she managed to forget about the gaping hole that Jerry had left in her life, all it took was running into someone she knew or who knew her story to remind her.

The head tilt.

The sympathetic smile.

The "How are you holding up?"

This pregnancy would only make those painful encounters a million times worse. And she was still struggling to wrap her head around the situation herself.

A newborn at thirty-nine.

Alone.

Beneath Gemma's hand, her belly fluttered and then settled.

A reluctant, bittersweet smile tugged at her lips. Okay, so not exactly alone. But parenting her two boys without Jerry was hard enough -- and they were in school. Full-time childcare, for free. Parenting two kids and a *newborn*? The smile dropped off her face as quickly as it had appeared.

How the hell was she going to do this?

Owen and Lena walked in with more boxes, and Gemma dropped her hand. She was wearing one of Jerry's old button down shirts, and her baby bump was still small, but that loose-fitting clothes wouldn't conceal her growing belly much longer. If this pregnancy was like her other two, she was a couple weeks from popping, and there would be no hiding it.

It was time to come clean...

She shot a glance at her brother as he set a box on the dining room table.

Just the thought of saying the words out loud filled her with dread and she swallowed them back.

A few more days, just to get settled in.

Ollie came bounding in through the still-open door, and Gemma leaned down to pet him. No one had ever called to claim the golden retriever they'd found at the park a few weeks back, and she couldn't bear to break her boys' hearts all over again by taking the beautiful dog to the pound. Besides, he was company for her through the long days that Liam and

Aiden spent at school. And so far, they had done a beautiful job of taking care of him. Liam walked him early each morning, and Aiden fed him before they went to meet the bus. After school, they took him to a park just around the corner where he could run and play with other dogs. Ollie had lucked out.

"There's no mattress in the master bedroom," Owen said. "The renters threw the old one away when they moved in, and took their own mattress with them when they moved. If you can't find a place that delivers, I can pick one up for you in my truck."

"It's okay," Gemma said, "I'm not in a rush. I can sleep in the bottom bunk in Aiden's room until I find a good one." Since Jerry's death, her younger son had been wanting her to stay in the room until he fell asleep, and Gemma sympathized. She had a hard time falling asleep alone in her room, too.

"We didn't know which boxes went to which kid," Lena said, "or which rooms they'd claimed, for that matter, so we just set the bedroom stuff on the living room for now."

"Thanks, that's perfect."

"It's lucky the yard has a fence," Owen said as Ollie went racing out the kitchen door in pursuit of a squirrel he'd caught sight of. Her brother shot his girlfriend a wide grin. "Remember my mam's basset hounds?"

"Yup. Sweet Bertie." Lena laughed. "I also remember the puppies."

Even Gemma cracked a smile. "How could you forget? There were *fifteen* of them!"

"But she found homes for them," Owen said. "Every one. Two of them went all the way down to Connecticut, and she drove another to Vermont herself. I still see some of the others around town... or I used to. I don't suppose any of them are alive anymore."

"Must be the grandbabies," Lena said.

Gemma felt a sudden spasm of grief.

She had spent so many sleepless nights thinking about how Jerry would never get to meet this baby, and she had often mourned the fact that her mother hadn't gotten more time with Liam and Aiden... but this was the first time it really hit her that this baby would never ever get to meet her mother. There was still Jerry's mother, at least. His parents weren't too far away... though they hadn't come to visit since she'd moved back to Maine. Maybe when she told them about the new baby...

That thought sent a wave of panic through her and she shoved it back.

"How are the boys liking school?" Lena asked. She was bustling about the kitchen, putting new liners in the drawers and putting away what few items Gemma had brought with her through all three of her recent moves. It was a moment before Lena's question registered.

"They like it, thank God," Gemma replied. "They're doing well."

Much better than they'd done at the school in Massachusetts that they'd attended for just a few weeks after Jerry died. Gemma shouldn't have put them in school at all, but it had seemed the thing to do. She had still imagined that she'd be able to function well enough to keep her new job. But it had been a failure, on every level. Gemma never wanted to set foot in that state again. It had stolen her husband, her future, her whole life, and then spit her back out.

"Are they making friends?" Lena asked.

Gemma blinked and pulled her attention back to the present.

"Actually, they are." She swallowed, took a deep breath, and forced herself to keep talking. "You know Aiden, he makes friends wherever he goes. He's already gotten a few birthday party invitations... though maybe at this age they're still inviting the whole class. I don't know. We have an invite from a family across the street, a girl in his class who turns ten in a couple months." She could vaguely remember the days of being organized and optimistic enough to send out invitations that far in advance...

"And Liam?" Lena asked. "Has he found kids his age to play with?"

"He has." It had been a struggle for her introverted twelve-year-old, but he had eventually connected with a boy in his grade who liked the same books and shows that he did. "He's planning to go to a friend's house on Friday for a sleepover."

"That's great! I know it's a hard age to move schools..." Lena skirted the fact that this was their third school this grade -- and the fact that they'd been dealt a far more traumatic blow than a move just a few months before. Just as well. Lena's fumbling but sweet encouragement was better than the heavy sympathy of Gemma's old classmates and acquaintances around Cherry Blossom Point. Her first week home, she'd almost been tempted to go back to Colorado. They had such a wonderful community there, friends that Liam and Aiden had known their whole lives. Her own friends in Denver had urged her to move back after the accident. But despite the happy years that Gemma had spent there -- just over two decades, in fact -- she knew that Denver wouldn't feel like home without Jerry. The boys must have felt the same, because they were never enthusiastic about the idea. Maine was better. They adored their uncle, and not having to pay rent lifted a huge portion of the stress that Gemma carried.

She still had no idea what she was going to do for work, or for child care, though. She had been lucky enough to stay home with her boys for over three years. Maybe if she worked from home, she could pay a mother's helper to come in during the day and tend to the new baby here. A retired neighbor in the mornings, say, and a teenage girl in the afternoon...two part-time employees just looking to learn a little extra money and cuddle a baby while Gemma worked. Anything was possible, right?

"Gem?"

She snapped back to the present just in time to catch the worried look on Owen's face. He had probably been talking to her for a while. She knew it concerned him, her silence these past months. Lena too. But Gemma couldn't help it. Worries swirled inside of her like a torrential storm, and every spoken word cost her a great deal of effort. She, who had been voted "most outgoing" in eighth grade. Gemma could hardly remember that girl.

"Sorry," she said to her brother. "I didn't hear you."

"I asked if you're planning to use Da's old den as a home office. Should I put your computer and books in there?"

"Sure." Gemma held it together long enough for Owen to

turn and walk away, then sank into one of the dining room chairs.

If the den was going to be an office, what would she use for a nursery? The baby's things could all go in her room, she supposed. It wasn't as if she and Jerry--

Oh, God.

Gemma's vision narrowed and she felt suddenly suffocated by this stuffy, old-fashioned dining room.

She put her head between her knees, fighting to catch her breath.

How was she going to raise a baby without him? Up all night with no one to tag her out in the morning. Worrying over every little cough or sneeze without Jerry there to talk her down. Who would bring her water when she was stuck beneath a sleepy, nursing baby? Who would cook for Liam and Aiden when she was too tired to function? How was she going to be able to afford to support three kids, plus pay for five years of childcare? An extra *decade* of parenting all on her own.

She couldn't do it.

She couldn't do this alone.

Lena crouched down beside her and laid a hand on her shoulder.

"Gemma? Sweetie, are you okay?"

Gemma sat up and nodded, but she couldn't stop the tears that streamed down her face when she sat up. That nod turned into a shake of her head as she met the other woman's gaze.

"Gemma?" Lena's voice was soft. "What's wrong?"

She took a deep breath and got her tears well enough

under control to choke out the two words she had been holding onto for weeks.

"I'm pregnant."

Check out the rest of Gemma's story, available for pre-order now or free upon release with kindle unlimited!

ALSO BY CHRISTINE GAEL

Want to get an alert next time a new book is out, find out about sales or contests, and chat with Christine? Join the mailing list **here!**

Maeve's Girls

(Standalone Women's Fiction)

Bluebird Bay

Finding Tomorrow

Finding Home

Finding Peace

Finding Forever

Finding Forgiveness

Finding Acceptance

Finding Redemption

Finding Refuge

Cherry Blossom Point

Starting From Scratch

Just Getting Started

A Fresh Start

A Head Start

Lucky Strickland Series (Mystery/Thriller)

Lucky Break

Getting Lucky

Crow's Feet Coven (Paranormal Women's Fiction)

Writing Wrongs

Brewing Trouble

Stealing Time

Made in the USA
Middletown, DE
17 November 2021